JAIL BAIT

It was bad luck for Mark Preston when he found Benny Hall murdered. Benny was Family, and dangerous people were involved. Hired by one faction and under threat from another, Preston found himself in a twilit world of blue movies and child prostitutes. A young schoolgirl was missing, and he had to find her. He also had to find the killer. Bodies began to pile up, and Rourke of Homicide was blaming Preston. The one bright spot was a racehorse. Its name? The Loser.

PETER CHAMBERS

JAIL BAIT

Complete and Unabridged

LINFORD
Leicester

First published in Great Britain in 1983

First Linford Edition
published 2003

British Library CIP Data

Chambers, Peter, *1924 –*
    Jail bait.—Large print ed.—
Linford mystery library
1. Detective and mystery stories
2. Large type books
I. Title
823.9'14 [F]

ISBN 0–7089–4922–3

Published by
F. A. Thorpe (Publishing)
Anstey, Leicestershire

Set by Words & Graphics Ltd.
Anstey, Leicestershire
Printed and bound in Great Britain by
T. J. International Ltd., Padstow, Cornwall

This book is printed on acid-free paper

1

It's a funny thing, the way a man can go through life and nobody knows he's there. But as soon as somebody puts two small pieces of metal into his heart, he suddenly makes the headlines. That's the way it was with little Benny Hall. Not that I knew his name at the beginning. He was just a little guy stretched out on the carpet, half-in and half-out of the elevator, so the doors couldn't close.

The man next to me must have been reading my mind.

'Tough way to get your name in the papers,' he observed.

'Right,' I agreed. 'You know him?'

He seemed to withdraw slightly.

'Know him? Why should I know him? I'm just a man who came to catch an elevator.'

'What's that?' snapped the uniformed cop, who was trying to keep order until help arrived. 'Did you say you know this man?'

He was looking at my companion, who shook his head angrily.

'Not me. Never seen him before. Better ask this guy. He was here before me.'

The officer transferred his gaze to me.

'That's right? You found the body?'

Other eyes were turning towards me now, nervous, hostile, suspicious. It made me jumpy.

'Find him? No, I didn't find him. That was the other man, the one who phoned in.'

My neighbour took a positive step to one side.

'There wasn't any other man when I got here, officer. Just this one here.'

The cop let his hand rest negligently on the flap of his gun holster.

'That right?'

'Certainly it's right,' I snapped irritably. 'I just told you, the other man went to telephone.'

'Yeah? Then where's he now? Did he come back? Is he one of these people?'

The growing knot of people in the

hallway began inspecting each other for signs of recent telephone calls. But the cop had a point. My man was not among them.

'I don't see him,' I admitted.

A little more unobtrusive shuffling, and we now had a clear tableau, instead of a disorderly mob. Most of those present dropped into the role of bystander, leaving three main characters. There was the dead man on the floor, the avenging angel, in the person of the cop, and the personification of evil, in the person of me. It was fairly clear from the surrounding faces that if the cop took it into his head to gun me down, that would be O.K. with them. That's what was needed around this town, a little more of the old rough justice, so a man could catch an elevator without somebody like me bumping him off.

The crowd made way for some newcomers, and a welcome voice said

'Well, well, look who's here.'

I turned gratefully towards the glowering countenance of Detective Second Grade Schultz, of the Homicide Bureau.

'Am I gad to see you, Schultzie — ' I began.

'I'll get to you later,' he interrupted. Then, rounding on the beat officer he said 'What's the tale, Pat?'

The tension was gone from the air. I leaned against the wall and poked an Old Favorite in my face. My recognition of Schultz seemed to make a profound impression on my late accusers. They were now nudging and whispering to each other, wondering about me, who I was, what I did, what put me on name terms with people from Homicide. My recent role of gunman was quickly forgotten, to be replaced by my new persona as undercover man, government agent or whatever.

Schultz's assistants started to circulate, taking down names and addresses, and the crowd melted gradually away. The media had arrived, and the scene-of-crime squad, with their tapes and cameras and the rest of the paraphernalia. A man knelt by the body, feeling pockets.

'Is there a room we could borrow?'

Schultz was addressing a nervous-looking man, who turned out to be the building manager.

'Oh certainly. Right this way.'

We all trooped behind him as he led us to a small office at the end of the corridor.

'This will be fine,' grunted Schultz, 'thank you for your cooperation. We'll try not to be too long.'

There were three chairs in the room, and five of us to be accommodated. Schultz sat down, beside a table covered with cardboard boxes. I grabbed one of the other chairs, and the others stood around, undecided.

'All right, Preston, what's it all about?'

I shrugged.

'How would I know? I went to catch the elevator. There was this dead guy — '

'Who said he was dead?' snapped an assistant.

I stared at him sadly.

'Let me explain something to you, sonny. It'll be of great help to you in your future career with the department. When you find a man lying on the ground, and then technicians start measuring him up, and three officers from the Homicide Squad appear on the scene, you can proceed on the assumption that you are dealing with a dead man.'

His face began to mottle and he said nastily

'Listen, you — '

'Cut it out,' said Schultz tiredly. 'What is it with you Preston, you have to annoy people all the time? All right, so you found this dead guy. What did you do?'

'I didn't say I found him,' I contradicted. 'There was this other man there. He said something about the man being dead, and he'd go call the police, and would I stay there.'

'Just like that?'

'Just like that.'

'Describe him.'

Schultz looked at me flatly, the cold eyes devoid of expression.

'Well, let's see, he was thirty-five or forty, light complexion, height around five nine, five ten, medium build. Yes, that would about cover it.'

The whistling sound like escaping

steam was the expulsion of air through Schultz's teeth.

'You forgot his name.'

'He didn't tell me his name,' I demurred.

'Oh yes he did. John Doe, that's his name. There's five million guys out there who fit that description. Can't you be more specific? Wasn't there anything about this guy at all?'

I sighed.

'Oh yes, I almost forgot.'

The assistants all looked at each other knowingly. Now we were coming to the facts. Schultz did not join in. I made them wait before continuing.

'Yes, I almost forgot the wooden leg. Man had a wooden leg, and a heavy brass ear-ring dangling at shoulder level — '

'Enough already. Don't give me a hard time, Preston. I came on duty fourteen hours ago, and the last thing I need is jokes. What I need is to go home and get to bed. You have a choice. You can either talk straight right now, or you can sit in a nice air-conditioned cell, and wait until I report back. That could be tonight, or it could be tomorrow morning. What's it gonna be?'

A homicide cop is always tough, but a homicide cop who's practically sleep-walking is as mean as a rattlesnake who missed breakfast.

'I came to this building on business. It was when I went to leave that I found this man in the corridor, crouching by the body. I thought somebody had passed out, nothing more. Then we had the chatter about calling in the police, then it just snowballed. Members of the public rolled up, just like always, then the beat cop arrived. That's it.'

There was a snort from one of the standing assistants, but I ignored it. Schultz was in no mood for sideshows. He nodded impartially.

'What were you doing here? Apart from running into murders.'

'I was working. There's a bond-jumper on the loose, and I had a call from San Francisco. The guy might be working for an outfit called AB Enterprises, here in Monkton. AB Enterprises has an office in this building, so I came to see them. It

8

was a bum lead as it happens, but I always have to check.'

He smiled, but there was no warmth in it. Wintry, that would be the word.

'Let's see the picture,' he suggested.

'Picture?'

That produced a sigh.

'Is that ear troubling you again? You say you came here on a skip trace job. That means there has to be flier on the man. And you must have a photograph if you want to get results. Let's have a look at it.'

I pulled out the envelope from inside my coat, and handed it over. Schultz opened it carefully, read the leaflet, and stared at the picture attached.

'You mean to tell me somebody trusted this face on a bond policy? I wouldn't let him near my kid's piggy bank. Horace Winters. No, I don't know him. Any of you guys know him?'

He passed around the likeness of the errant Horace. One of the standers said

'I don't know him, but I'd arrest a guy who looked like that, just on appearances.'

I held out my hand for the papers.

'One thing in his favor,' I submitted. 'He does make life easy for people like me. Nobody makes a mistake about whether they've seen him or not.'

But Schultz had lost interest.

'All right Preston, go away. And stop finding bodies. It gives people a bad impression.'

I didn't need to be told twice. At the door I said

'By the way, who was the dead man?'

'Not that it's any of your business,' was the sour reply, 'but his name is Benjamin Hall. Does it mean anything?'

'No,' I admitted. 'From out of town, is he?'

'Preston, right now there are two doors available to you. One is on a nice cosy cell. The other is behind you.'

The one behind me had no bars on it. I went out quickly, pulling it to.

'Ah, a development.'

There was a little knot of people standing around in the corridor. I knew several of them by sight, and the rest all fitted the same general pattern. The fourth estate had arrived, fearless protectors of the public interest. The man who greeted me was Tip Hatch of the Sentinel.

'What's going down, Preston? Why'd they let you go? Was it self-defense?'

I held up a protecting hand, but not fast enough to prevent a couple of cameras from flashing.

'I just happened to be around,' I protested. 'There's no story here.'

'Haw, haw,' jeered Hatch. 'For the benefit of anybody who happens to be new on the crime beat, permit me to introduce Mr. Mark Preston, private investigator of this city. He just happens to be around when people get deceased.'

I wondered for a moment why he said that. It isn't like a newspaper-man to give out free information to the competition. Then I worked it out. Everybody there knew me. Everybody, that is, except a bright-eyed girl I'd never seen before. She had to be new, and Hatch was showing off for her benefit. Not that I blamed him, she certainly justified a little showing off.

'What paper are you with, honey?' I asked.

'No paper, Mr. Preston. I'm free-lancing for the syndicates. I'm Sue-Ellen Denison.'

'Tell you what, Sue-Ellen,' I suggested, 'why don't we go talk privately some place? I could give you an exclusive.'

This produced a chorus of derisive howls.

'Put her down Preston, we were here first,' growled Hatch. 'And don't change the subject. Why did you bump off this Hall? Was it an argument over a dame?'

I winked at Sue-Ellen, and pushed my way through. After the cool of the building, the sudden glare of the outside sun made an unhappy contrast. It was no time for a man to be out pounding concrete. It was a time for cool shady bars and the sound of ice-cold beer shushing softly into frosted glasses. As it happened, I knew of just such a place, and I lost no time in making my way there. The story goes that a woman once set foot in Sam's Bar, and many's the time I've listened to speculation about what happened on that historic occasion. I didn't see her, and I don't know anybody else who did, but the tale persists. People just won't let go of a good tale. She certainly wasn't around today. It was the usual crowd, mostly business guys catching an early lunch.

Sam nodded to me, pulling up a mug of frothy suds and sliding it across. I went and parked against the far wall, acknowledging familiar faces on the way, avoiding conversation. I didn't feel like talking to anybody. What I needed was a chance to sit and think about life, and its general relationship to one Preston M.

It was a nuisance, not having put the arm on Horace Winters. That would have brought in a nice cash sum, and cash sums were very prominent in my thoughts at that time. I had recently made a discovery of some special importance, but it was costing me a lot of money. You sometimes hear people say they wonder whatever became of all the horses that used to pull the ice-carts and garbage waggons through the city streets. I had come up with the answer. What they did was, they put leather saddles on them, gave them fancy names. Then they took them out to Palmtrees race track, and told people they were racehorses. A lot of people believed this, including the Preston M. I mentioned, and bet their hard-earned money on these fleabags. Just the day before, one of them was actually placed third, until the stewards realised he'd been overtaken by the first two horses in the race following the one he was supposed to be running in.

These days, you hear a lot of people winding on about something called cash flow. I don't know much about the business world, but I get the impression it means there's more cash flowing out than there is flowing in, and that I understand very well. All my cash was flowing out to the bookmakers, and if I didn't get some flowing in the reverse direction, my relationship with the bank manager was apt to become strained.

'Saddle me bags if it ain't Mr. Preston.'

I looked up, to see the unhappy features of Mournful Harris. He is a long, cadaverous streak of a man who looks like a foretaste of impending doom. Which he frequently is. Mournful is what is called a tipster. That is to say, he touts around the horse-players, bearing this secret inside information. He will give you the word on the outcome of a certain race, the idea being that you cut him in for a piece of the action. If the horse wins, he collects. If it doesn't, he goes out of sight for a while, and next time you see him, he has a complicated tale about what went wrong.

''Lo, Mournful.'

He swivelled his eyes from side to side, to ensure we were not being overheard.

'Got a little something for you. O.K. to sit?'

The question was only a formality. He was sitting down as he put it. We had some more eye-swivelling, plus a little added head-rolling for extra conviction.

'I wouldn't want this to go any further,' he opened.

I shrugged.

'You got it. Just don't tell me about it, and your secret is safe.'

He continued to add yet another fold of skin over his heavily creased and lined face, to indicate hurt.

'Look, Mr. Preston, did I ever steer you wrong?'

The man should have been a politician. Over the years, he had slipped me a handful of winners, among dozens of escapees from the glue-factory. And yet, to look at that woebegone countenance, you would think he was the all-time victim of misunderstanding.

I sighed.

'Do you want me to read the list? I have it here someplace.'

'Listen,' he begged, 'I been a little unlucky once or twice — '

' — huh — '

' — once or twice,' he repeated, 'but this here stuff I'm carrying right now, it's dynamite.'

'Then you shouldn't be smoking.'

He'd been reaching out for the pack of Old Favorites, which I had carelessly left within grasping distance. I edged it neatly away as I spoke.

He sighed, and dropped his voice even lower.

'Now hear this. What would you say if I told you I had certain information about a switch job?'

I paused, with the beer-glass halfway to

16

my face. This might prove to be something after all.

The switch is almost as old as horse-racing itself. What happens is this. A quality horse is entered in some unimportant race under a false name. The name usually belongs to an unsuccessful plodder, and long odds are laid against it. There is no heavy betting in advance, because this would draw attention to the horse, and, in any case the odds would drop. A few minutes before post-time, the smart money is laid on the switch-horse, but even then this is spread around all over the country. There is no giant bet in one place to attract attention. The horse romps home, everybody says well, who would have thought it, and bets are paid. By the time people are able to get their heads together, the horse is back in its own stable, under its own name, and the change cannot be proven. It is a very old dodge, and very risky, but the profits are so enormous that it still goes on.

'You seem to be listening, Mr. Preston.'

Mournful's sad tones drifted across the table.

'I'm listening,' I admitted.

'Friday. The third race,' he went on.

'Does he have a name?'

He spread his bony hands in a gesture of deference.

'This is kind of one-sided,' he suggested.

What he meant was, what was in it for him. Usually I would put him down for five dollars, ten if I was in an expansive mood. A switch would certainly qualify for ten.

'I'll put in ten for you.'

Now he was horrified.

'Mr. Preston, this is not just some tip I'm giving you here. This is red hot information. Money in the bank. Like the key to Fort Knox. I'm sorry, but ten won't do at all.'

If the story was true, he was right of course.

'What are the odds?'

'Twelve to one,' he supplied.

'So how much do you figure this is worth?'

'It has to be half a yard. I'm not telling anybody else. Just one man. You.'

'Fifty bucks?' I tried to sound more

affronted than I felt. He was quite right. It was money in the bank. 'I'm going to be quite upset if anything goes wrong, but O.K. Fifty it is.'

He nodded, satisfied.

'The Loser,' he whispered.

'What?'

'That's the name. The Loser.'

Great. Yet it made a kind of sense. Nobody was going to bet any money on a name like that.

'All right, Mournful, we have a deal. No doubt I'll be seeing you Friday night. Where'll you be?'

He stood up, and the way his mouth moved around told me there was a smile somewhere along the creases.

'Don't worry about it. I'll find you.'

I didn't doubt that. A tout with money to come can home in on the source like a racing pigeon.

A racing pigeon. It was an unfortunate analogy, and I sincerely hoped it had no relevance to my new situation.

Finishing up my drink, I was about to leave when my way was suddenly blocked by Tip Hatch.

'Thought I'd find you here.'

'So you found me,' I grunted. 'And I still don't know anything about the murder.'

He nodded quizzically.

'I hope that's true Preston, for your sake. There's going to be a lot of people upset about this. Do you know who that guy was?'

'Benjamin Hall? No, I never heard of him. You tell me.'

The sharp eyes inspected me as he replied.

'Not Benjamin,' he corrected. 'Beniamino. A real family man. His relatives are going to be upset.'

That was bad news indeed. But not for me. If this Beniamino Hall or whatever was a syndicate operator, it was no skin off my nose. I was just a passing stranger, and it was nothing to do with me.

You'd think I'd have learned by now.

2

I went back to the office. Florence Digby was seated at her desk, staring at the small screen of the word-processor, as information spaced itself out in neat lines for inspection. As I entered, she looked up, pressing the Hold button.

'Ah, Mr. Preston,' she greeted crisply, 'did you have any luck with Mr. Winters?'

I shook my head.

'No. They never heard of him. We had a little excitement down there. Man got himself killed.'

She shed about two per cent of her cool detachment.

'Really? What happened?'

I told her the tale, what there was of it.

'The police thought at first his name was Benjamin Hall, but I ran into Hatch of the Sentinel later, and he told me the Benjamin should have read Beniamino.'

'And the Hall?' she queried.

'Huh?'

That brought me one of her patient smiles.

'People don't just Americanise one half of their names. He made Benjamin out of Beniamino, but what did he make Hall out of?'

I hadn't bothered to think that far, but she was right.

'See what you mean,' I grunted. 'Still, it doesn't have to concern me. He meant nothing to me alive, and I really can't start working up any interest now he's dead. Did anything new come in?'

Florence shook her head. 'Not a thing. I'm having a lovely time, storing all our old records in these memory banks. By the time I'm finished, we'll be able to get rid of a lot of paper around here.'

The word-processor was her new toy, and she was determined to make the most of it. I wasn't yet completely sold.

'Before you start junking anything, I'd like to go through it. Some of that stuff is irreplaceable.'

I went through to my own office, and parked behind the empty desk. Florence had finally beaten me down about installing her new machinery, after months of steady argument. It had set me back over ten thousand plus extras that everybody conveniently forgot about when negotiations began. I didn't like the idea of losing my records. I didn't doubt the new gizmo would retrieve all the vital information, and in fact I knew it would, because I'd seen it in action. But there's nothing to hold in the hand. Sometimes, just looking through an old report can bring back to mind the circumstances under which it was put together. Staring at a piece of paper for the tenth time can suddenly produce a recognition flash, which didn't happen in the first nine looks. I wasn't convinced I would get the same experience looking at a glass screen, nor at the flimsy print-out that went with it. Besides, and I didn't want to bother Florence Digby with the prospect, if things didn't begin to cheer up on the financial front, her new pet might find itself heading back to the toyshop.

Standing by the window I stared out towards the Pacific. The blue Pacific, I should have said, apologies to the Tourist

Bureau. They would have been pleased with the ocean today. It was sparkling fresh under the hot sun, gentle waves breaking in orderly white lines as they advanced towards the golden beach. Small boats bobbed around, with bright sails contributing to the general technicolor effect. A few lunatics were actually splashing around in the water, while more sensible people stretched out on loungers, gently sweating it out. The most sensible people of all of course were not on view at all. They were tucked away on cool shady verandahs, with tall frosted glasses to hand, and maybe a tall frosted blonde to go with everything else.

That's what sensible people were doing. Not tracking around the city, chasing ugly faces like Horace Winters. Not finding corpses in every doorway, and being harangued by police officers. I got to thinking about Horace. He'd been smart enough to persuade his employers to trust him, smart enough to disappear with the take. Wasn't it a reasonable assumption that a man that smart would have sense enough to stay out of the sun?

Wasn't it feasible that old Horace was out there right now, parked in one of the beach bars, quietly enjoying his illicit gains? And wouldn't it be a reasonable thing for a private investigator to go searching in those bars, taking aboard the occasional iced beer as a kind of cover?

It would, I decided.

It was no more than my plain duty to get down to the beach haunts. After all, Horace Winters was certainly not going to march into my office and give himself up. How could he? It was unlikely he'd ever heard of me. No, the more I thought about it, the more my next step became clear. I had no right to be twiddling my thumbs behind a desk, while my quarry sat in a cool bar, laughing at me. It was a nice piece of rationalisation, and the kind I can modestly claim to be rather good at. The decision made, I was about to cross the room when Florence Digby came in, bearing paper.

'I think I've got him,' she announced triumphantly.

'Winters?' I nodded. 'Yes, I was just thinking — '

'Not Winters,' she cut in. 'Hall. Your friend Hall.'

Personally, I don't consider that a sight of a man's dead body entitles me to claim his friendship, but I let it pass.

'What about him?'

I might as well ask the question, because nothing was going to prevent her from telling me.

'I think he's one of the Halsetti family. Look at this.'

I didn't want to look at this. I knew enough at second hand about the Halsetti crowd to make me avoid any first-hand information. But there was no stopping Florence.

She spread out a chart on the desk, and I leaned over with reluctance. Florence is an organisation nut. Every time a kid sticks up a cigar store, she tries to point up syndicate connections. The paper on display was an intricate hotch-potch of boxes and lines, with place-names and family names in a bewildering web. The cities at the top bore far-off names. Detroit, Cleveland, Chicago and many more passed under my eye. Florence was stabbing away with a manicured forefinger down in the right-hand corner.

'There you are,' she announced triumphantly. 'Halsetti.'

Skipping the rest, I looked at where she was pointing. The legend read 'Robert Halsetti b. 1910'. The nearest place name was San Francisco. At least it was closer.

'No good,' I decided. 'The man's in his seventies, if he's still alive. Besides, the name is wrong.'

Florence tutted.

'You have to follow the lines downward.'

I did that and found that Robert had three sons, none of them named Beniamino. There were no more lines.

'Nice try Florence, but it isn't working. There's no Beniamino listed there, and besides, who says the name has to be Halsetti? There have to be a dozen other Italian names you could abbreviate down to Hall.'

Sensing that I wasn't going to buy her theory, Florence arched her back stiffly, and began carefully to refold the precious chart.

'A dozen at least,' she agreed. 'Could

you suggest two? Or even one, as a starter?'

'Well, theres — there's — ' I gave it up. 'Hell, I don't know. Try our immigration section.'

She sniffed with evident satisfaction.

'Just as I thought. I'll bet it turns out I'm right.'

I shrugged wearily.

'It really doesn't matter, one way or the other. Mr. Hall is of no interest to me. The man who does interest me is Winters. Horace Winters, remember? I'm going to take a ride out, see if I can get a line on him.'

'Whatever will you say. Where will you try next?'

She has the damnedest way of looking at me when she suspects my motives. Like now. I avoided her eye.

'Public places,' I said off-handedly. 'Though I might try the beach.'

'Huh.'

And with that she flounced out. Flouncing is strictly a female pastime, and Florence Digby is up there with the big flouncers, when it's flouncing time.

When I passed her desk on the way out, she was pretending to be engrossed in the glass screen again. I made my way down to the underground parking lot, glad of the dark coolness down there. Unlocking the Chev, I was about to climb in when arms came around me from both sides, locking my own helplessly in place. Except that I was unable to move, nobody tried to hurt me.

'Mr. Preston?' said a voice over my shoulder.

'What the hell do you guys think you're doing?' I protested, trying to squirm against the iron locks.

'You are Mr. Preston?' invited the voice.

The use of that 'Mr.' was intriguing, mad as I was.

'Yes, I'm Preston,' I admitted, 'and I doubt if there's fifty dollars on me.'

That brought me a soft laugh, not unpleasant.

'Your money is safe. Somebody wants to have a chat with you.'

I tried to turn my head, to get a look at my captors, but one of them had a fist like a sandbag pressed against the back of my neck.

'Just take it easy,' came the whispered advice. 'There isn't far to go.'

The next thing I knew was the sound of a car drawing up close behind me. A door clicked smoothly open, and I was being lifted backwards, and then pushed, not urgently, into the rear seat. At once a man climbed in either side of me, and the doors were shut tight. One of them tapped on the black glass dividing up from the driver, and we rolled smoothly away. The black glass was all around us, and that, coupled with the enormous dark glasses favored by my new friends, effectively prevented me from getting a good look at them. All I knew was they were young, powerfully built and dark-haired. They pressed companionably against me from each side, as if to emphasise there wasn't to be any sudden lunging around from me. The car smelled of leather and cigar smoke, with soft carpeting and expensive fittings. It was the kind of car used by very wealthy people, and also, I reminded myself, by another kind of people.

Less than a minute had elapsed since I fitted my key in the car-door. These people knew their business, they were professionals. The thought did nothing to calm my jangled nerves.

'All right,' I said, surprised to find my voice pitched two tones above normal. 'So I'm here. What happens now.'

The reply came from my left, and it was the same man who'd spoken earlier.

'Now we can all relax and enjoy the ride,' he advised smoothly.

'I like to know where I'm riding,' I snapped. 'Who are you guys?'

The man on my right seemed to stiffen a little, and I half expected him to take a poke at me. But it was still his companion who did the talking.

'We are just messengers,' he informed me. 'There's a man who wants to see you.'

'I have an office,' I said plaintively.

He chuckled, in that pleasant way he had.

'This man doesn't go to see people. They go to see him.'

And that was the end of the conversation. It was obvious I wasn't going to get anything out of these two goons. It was clear, too, that whoever I was going to see was someone of importance. Hoodlums of this calibre don't come cheap. Then there was the car, and a third man to drive it. Somebody was going to a lot of expense just to see me. But why? All he had to do was pick up a telephone, and I would have gone anyway.

We were clear of the city now, and rolling northwards behind the line of hills that run parallel with the coastline.

'O.K. Mr. Preston, just kneel down on the floor, will you?'

'What for?'

There was that shifting around again, from the right. The talker said

'Just a little precaution. Or you could have a blindfold, if you prefer.'

I did not prefer. If these people didn't want me to see where I was going, that was all right with me. Dropping forward, I knelt on springy carpet, keeping my head low. This went on for a while, then the car slowed, and was turning gently to the left. I began to raise my head, but the sandbag was there, keeping it firmly lowered. Finally we stopped moving, and I could hear the unmistakeable sound of closing hydraulic doors.

'O.K. Mr. Preston, out.'

It isn't easy to make a dignified exit from a car, when you start out from a kneeling position. I kind of half-shuffled and half-groped my way outside. We were in a large garage, with two other cars on view, and room for more.

'This way.'

My senior captor led the way up some stone steps to a door, and opening it, passed through. Behind me, the non-talker gave me a gentle shove to get me started. I went up, trying to make a mental picture of the layout, in case I had to make a run for it. At the same time I knew I was only kidding myself. Already there were three men to deal with, four counting the one who wanted to see me. I wasn't going anywhere unless they said so. It did nothing for my ego, and less for my temper.

The door led into a hallway, a spacious

area with heavy carpets scattered around, and some nice pieces of oak furniture. Through the windows I could see well-tailored lawns, and neat ornamental shrubbery. There was even a fountain. My host was evidently a man of means, whatever else he might turn out to be.

I wasn't kept long before finding out. A pair of fancy doors stood open, and my guards stood each side, motioning me in. I went hesitantly forward, and into a large comfortable room with a huge Spanish fireplace dominating one side. Not that I saw it at first. My attention was all for the man who stood watching my entrance.

Not very tall, he probably tipped five feet eight inches, but that took time to register. He was broad like a tree, with massive shoulders and a barrel chest that radiated primitive strength, and something else. Authority. This man was in charge. As to his age, he could have been anything between forty and fifty. The face was wide and fleshy, spoiled by tiny eyes in deep creased recesses, eyes that were black and bored into a man. He had a smile like a steel trap.

'Mr. Preston, it was nice you could come. Appreciate that.'

It was on the tip of my tongue to give him an answer to that, but I managed to stop in time. We were into some kind of game, and I had better obey the rules. His rules.

'Well, it was one of those invitations,' I replied. 'You know the kind.'

Some of the smile shifted out to his jaws. It improved him.

'We'll get along,' he decided. 'Siddown, siddown.'

I saddown, but he remained standing. He didn't have to do that. He would dominate the conversation if he chose to lie on the floor.

'Seen you on the midday news,' he informed me. 'You look better in the flesh.'

'Oh?' and my surprise was not faked. 'I didn't realise I was on.'

The tiny eyes narrowed a little, then he nodded.

'It was just a little thing, just a few seconds. It was about you finding little

Benny Hall's body.'

I'd had a growing suspicion there might be some connection between that and my trip out to the country.

'Oh that,' I disclaimed. 'I was just passing by.'

'That's what they said,' he agreed. 'Only, you know how they are. You know the way they can say something, without coming right out and saying it.'

I knew what he meant, and our local tee vee station was very good at it. If you wrote down the actual words, or repeated them, especially in a courtroom, nothing exceptionable had been said. Simply facts, figures, straight reporting. But put together in a way that left the door open for viewers to put their own interpretation on what they meant. If they had been talking about the Benny Hall case, and then slipped in a few remarks about me, it wouldn't be hard for the watching audience to assume I knew more than I was telling.

'Something tells me I'm not going to like this, but please go on.'

He nodded.

'Yeah, well, I think you catch the drift. They said what a well-known guy you was in the detecting business. There was some chatter about one or two murders you been mixed up in. By the time they got through, it seemed like one helluva coincidence you happened to be around when little Benny cashed in.'

'And that's exactly what it was,' I stated flatly. 'That, and no more. I never heard of the man, till the police told me his name.'

He shrugged, and a couple of hundred-weight of steel muscle bounced and rippled around under the three hundred dollar grey charcoal suit.

'Maybe. Still, it made me curious. It still does. Tell me about it. Tell me how come you was there.'

Once again I had to restrain my immediate impulse. This was not some-body you told to go to hell. He had a special relationship with that destination, and had probably sent custom in that direction more than once. Stifling the angry retort, I held my self in check, and repeated calmly the story I'd given to

37

Schultz and his gang. There's something very soothing to the nerves about telling the truth. You don't have to watch out for snags and pitfalls all the time. You don't have to weigh up every word to see if it can lead you into trouble. There aren't any snags, and there isn't going to be any trouble. All you do is simply recite the facts. It's beautiful.

My host stood with head bent, not looking at me during my little recital. When I finished he said

'And that's all?'

'That's all.'

He was looking at me now.

'This Detective Schultz, now. Straight copper?'

'Like an arrow,' I said unhesitatingly, 'and just as sharp.'

'You was lucky he didn't toss you in the can, him being so tired and all.'

He wasn't making conversation. It was a direct question.

'He would have, if he thought I was holding out on him,' I explained. 'But Schultzie knows me. I'm not in the murder business, and I never heard of this

Hall until today.'

'Uh huh,' nodded my interrogator. 'And this other guy, the lamster, what was his name, Winters? Yeah Winters, you think you're going to find him?'

'I'm certainly going to try,' I assured him with feeling. 'There's fifteen hundred riding on his nose, and I could use it.'

That brought me a half-smile.

'You don't look like a man who's about to starve to death.'

I made a face.

'This business I'm in has patches. Things have been quiet for a while, and I have certain responsibilities. I'll be glad of the money.'

He moved suddenly, taking three strides to an upright padded chair opposite me, and lowering himself into it.

'Before I invited you along,' he informed me, 'I made a coupla calls. People I know in Monkton City. The way I hear it, the only responsibilities you have are dames and bookmakers. Do I hear right?'

'These things cost money,' I replied. 'Especially the bookies.'

'You want a job?'

He slipped the words out quietly, and without preamble. It was the last thing I had expected, and my face probably registered some surprise. This man, whoever he was, had organisation. I didn't see what I could do for him that his own people couldn't.

'That would depend on what it is,' I hedged. 'You've got people, you've got connections. And money. Where would I come in?'

'That is a fair question,' he conceded, 'and the answer is simple. You're asking me what could you do that my own people couldn't do, and the answer is, not much. I don't want you because of what you can do. I want you because of who you are. A loner, a man on his own. No connections. Everybody knows it, and that makes you special.'

There was a flaw in his reasoning, and I pointed it out.

'But if I started to work for you, that would give me connections.'

He slapped a vast hand against his thigh.

'Plus, you are smart. Let me explain to you what this is all about, but first you have to understand one thing. You repeat what I'm going to tell you, and you're dead. O.K.?'

I've been threatened before, and it doesn't bother me too much. But this was different. This wasn't a threat. It was a simple statement of fact. A program of forthcoming events. Suddenly, it was chilly in the room. I managed to say

'I hear you.'

It seemed to satisfy him.

'Good. Well then, this is how it shapes. There's certain people up in San Francisco in a certain way of business. They run it, the whole operation, and it's theirs. There's certain other people, down this end of the state, in the same way of business. That is theirs. If you like, it's mine. Now these two lots of people I'm telling you about, they keep out of each other's way. No trouble. Everybody knows what he's doing, where his territory starts and finishes. There hasn't been a gun go off in ten years. We all like it that way, and I'm going to see it stays that way. You with me so far?'

I could have wished I wasn't, but there was no mistaking what I was being told. It didn't help to know that Florence Digby had been right. This was family business, with a capital F.

'I have the picture,' I admitted glumly.

'O.K., so let's look at what we got here. This dead guy, this Hall, his proper monniker is Halsetti. Does that tell you anything?'

'No,' I lied.

'All right, then I'll tell you. The Halsettis ain't much. They're a small group of people mostly muscle and not much brain. But, and this is where it counts, they work for these other people up north. That gives these other people the responsibility. They have to look after them, right?'

'Right.'

He paused before continuing, as if to satsify himself I was paying attention. He needn't have worried. My ears were almost standing out.

'So what do we have?' he went on. 'Here's this Benny, even his own family

42

can't control him. He's an independent, picking up a buck here, a buck there. He's not much of anything at all, but he's still a Halsetti.'

He stopped again, looking at me hard. I thought we might save a little time.

'I think I see where you're heading. These friends of yours, up in San Francisco, they might wonder whether you have any idea what happened to this wandering boy. Is that it?'

His face was horrified.

'No,' he spat, 'that ain't it at all. None of my people would pull a dumb stunt like this, and nobody would think so. Whoever give it to Benny was an amateur. You must know that. Right in a public building, broad daylight. No, no. Here's how it shapes. Like I told you, these Halsettis ain't too long on brains. They're liable to come down here, waving guns around, upsetting people. That kind of thing can get out of hand. What I want to do is clean this up. I want the clown who killed Benny Hall, and I want him alive. I want him handed over to the law in a nice neat parcel. That's where you come in.

You're clean. You find this comedian, you grab him, you turn him in. Plenty of publicity, all good clean stuff, no talk about syndicates and all that old malarkey. What this is, one no-hoper gets himself rubbed out by another one. That's how it is, that's how it stays. You got the picture?'

Regrettably, I had.

'I understand what you're telling me,' I said carefully, 'but I don't know that I can guarantee results. As you said yourself, this is a real amateur setup. If Hall was killed by an ordinary citizen, it's going to be very hard to find him.'

'Hard is your problem,' was the matter-of-fact reply. 'The point is, you got the job. Here's a grand. There's five more when you get a result. But make it quick.'

An envelope was stuck under my nose. I didn't bother to open it. If this man said there was a thousand dollars inside, then that was the figure. And all the chatter about whether I wanted the job was just that. Chatter. I was hired, as of now, and I'd better get used to the idea.

'How will I contact you?' I asked.

'You know better than that,' he grunted. 'We'll be in touch.'

'I like to know who I'm working for,' I insisted.

The tiny black eyes were like marble.

'No problem. You're working for me. Remember it.'

The fact that he didn't have a name was not discussed.

I nodded and stood up.

'Well, I'm not getting paid to sit around here chewing the fat,' I announced. 'Do I get a ride back to town?'

He laughed then, a short, barking sound, which was somehow rusty. Maybe he didn't laugh very much.

'I got a feeling we'll get along,' he pronounced expansively. 'Sure, sure you get a ride back. And good luck to you.'

I tried some kind of smile, but it got no further than my teeth.

Five minutes later I was feeling that floor carpet again, in the rear of the giant Buick. They dropped me off outside the office, and rolled away without a word.

It was five-thirty on a hot steamy

evening, and the rest of the world was getting set to relax.

The rest of the world didn't have my problems.

3

Benny and me made the front page of the evening papers, pictures and all. I had the edge, because a man standing facing the camera always takes a better picture than a guy lying face down on the floor. The scribe managed to get a two-column spread out of it, which isn't bad when you consider all he had in the way of hard fact was a couple of names and addresses. I made a note of the late Mr. Hall's address, and read quickly what they had to say about me. There was nothing new, just the usual fluff about 'the well-known private investigator, blah blah'. Still, it made me uneasy. Maybe I worry too much, but the association of ideas was being planted for anybody who cared to look. A picture of a man who'd been murdered, and right next to him a picture of me. Anybody could be forgiven for associating the two together in his mind.

La Digby had gone home, leaving

messages on my desk. One was a note that Sam Thompson was available for any work I may have. The other said that Mr. Andrews, of Andrews Clark and Andrews, had called. He was sorry to have missed me at the office, and may try to reach me at home that evening. In any event he would certainly telephone again tomorrow. Florence had added the information that the firm were lawyers with a gold rating. That was good news. Lawyers, and especially gold-rated lawyers, usually meant work to someone like me, and I'd been a little short on work lately. True, I had this Hall case on my hands, but that wouldn't last very long. When mob people howl for action they usually get it. It isn't their style to hang around waiting for things to happen. They want results now, and if things don't move fast enough to suit them, they do a little moving on their own account. No, Mr. Andrews was a welcome caller, and I'd be interested to know what he wanted.

That left Thompson. I read Florence's note again. Mr. Thompson was now available, indeed. Do tell. What she meant was that Sam's private economic recession had now reached a point where he'd have to descend to doing some work. Sam is a loner, an individual even in these corporate days. All he asks is a place to sleep, and freedom to spend the rest of his life propping up bars, and philosophising with anybody who happens to be within earshot. Constitutionally there is nothing against his life-style, but economically it is unsound. A man can spend his money any way he wants, even these days, but that is always based on the assumption that he has some money in the first place. In these harsh times, the only way people can latch on to the essential bread is by getting involved in something called work, and that is where Sam's system lets him down. Sam has no love for work. In fact, it would not be taking things too far to say that Sam is something of a genius in avoiding that particular area. But booze costs money, and the day comes when even the most gullible of bartenders starts reaching under the counter for that baseball bat. When that happens, Sam takes stock, finds he doesn't have any, and calls my office. Strange thing, the man is good. He is smart and tough, and there is no one in town to match him as a leg-man. If only he could bring himself to line up with the rest of the citizens, he could have his own agency in no time. That would interfere with his drinking, of course, and that makes it nonviable.

I couldn't see where I could use him at that moment, but it was useful to know he was around.

My watch said it was now after six o'clock, and that meant the night editors would have swung into action on the newssheets. Locking up the office, I drove around to the Globe, parking the heap in the fashion editor's slot. Those ladies do not work nights. Then I walked into the usual uproar of a busy newspaper office. The man I wanted to see was Shad Steiner, the irascible night editor, and one of the most respected newspapermen on the entire coast.

He was huddled up as usual in the glass cubicle they called his office, tossing paper around in a seemingly haphazard way. Somehow or other, tomorrow's Globe would emerge from all this apparent chaos, and I'd never yet worked out how they did it.

'Mr. Steiner, sir.'

I knew that would make him look up, and it did. The criss-crossed face inspected me thoughtfully.

'The night editor's dream finally comes true,' he chortled. 'Killer surrenders to Globe. Bless you Preston, for selecting me for this honor, and believe me, the Globe will see to it you get a fair trial. There will be no railroading here. Just take a seat, and I'll have someone come in and take down your statement.'

I sank into the seat, raising a hand in protest.

'Knock if off Shad, I was just an innocent bystander.'

'Oh really? You could have fooled me. Did you see the midday news? They practically had you in the box.'

'So I hear,' I grumbled. 'Anyway, what were you doing watching? You should have been asleep.'

'Sleep,' he muttered absently, 'sleep. I

keep hearing that word, keep promising myself I'm going to look it up in the dictionary. It's something I know nothing about. Look, I'm busy, how about that confession?'

'No dice. But you were right, as usual, about the newscast. It did give people the wrong impression. Matter of fact, a couple of people said something to me. Wrong people.'

He scraped a pencil irritably down one side of his lined face, and tilted back in his chair.

'Wrong people?' he echoed. 'You mean mob guys? Do I smell a story? A gang war would be nice. All I have tomorrow is an impeached senator, and frankly, it's boring. If you could swing a few bullet-riddled bodies my way, it would be a favor.'

I nodded, as if thinking it over.

'I'll tell you Sam, the only bullet-riddled body I'm going to come up with is liable to be mine, and — '

' — don't knock it,' he interrupted. 'Make a nice tale. Fearless Investigator Victim of Gangland Vengeance. Beats the hell out of all this crap about committees of enquiry. What do you say?'

'I say shut up and let me finish,' I growled. 'This Hall case is getting to be a nuisance. People think I'm — mixed up in it — and I'm not — but they still think it. Hall seems to have had some connection with organised crime — '

' — huh — '

' — and today I had a message.'

His eyes didn't exactly gleam, but they certainly glowed.

'Tell me about the message.'

I looked at him very straight-faced.

'Two hoodlums stopped me on the street. They said it was a terrible thing, what happened to Benny Hall. They said they hoped I didn't know anything about it, because if I did Benny's friends would be calling to see me.'

'They said that?' he mused. 'Good. You want me to print it?'

'Not yet. I want to find out who those two were.'

'What for?' he snapped.

'So that I'll know the connection. Once I know who a man's friends are, I'm halfway to finding out his enemies. And — '

' — and maybe halfway to finding out who bumped him off,' finished Shad. 'Yes, that makes sense. So, you want to look at some pictures, see if you can spot your new friends. Right?'

'Right.'

The wise old eyes narrowed.

'Why here? They got better pictures at police headquarters.'

I put on a pained expression.

'Aw come on, Shad. You know how those people are. They'd probably keep me down there two days, trying to establish some connection. Anyway, it's bad for my image.'

' — didn't know you had an image,' was the sour interjection.

'Well, I do. I'm the fearless private investigator, remember? How's it gonna look if I go running to the law every time somebody slaps my wrist. And there's another reason.'

I left it hanging there, to see if he'd grab at it.

'Ah,' he nodded. 'Now we come to it.

Tell me about this other reason.'

'I want the Globe to know what I'm doing. Specifically, I want you to know.'

The pencil went to work again.

'Why?'

'Because if I should have a nasty accident, you would know what caused it. You might even be tempted to do something about it.'

He chewed on that for a moment.

'Don't see what I could do that the police couldn't. And they would do it better,' he objected.

'When they had something to go on,' I agreed. 'But they are busy people. They have unsolved crime coming out of their ears. They wouldn't give me any particular publicity, not without any evidence. It's not part of their job to keep reminding the public about cases which are still under investigation. You are different. You have to sell newspapers. You can put pressure on, and keep it on. Do I get to see the pictures?'

'You do,' he decided. 'So, for now, we keep quiet, right? But the moment you come up with something, I get it. Right?'

'Right.'

Five minutes later I was sitting in an empty room, with the Globe's special crime folders open on the table. Over these past few years, there has been a great blaze of publicity given to the organisation of criminal networks, and a lot of it has been good, factual material. But things and people change, and what was true five years ago is not necessarily true today. In an attempt to keep up-to-date, most of the newspapers maintain their own files, noting changes of personnel, shifts of influence and so forth. As a system, it isn't infallible, but like the man said, it's all there is.

One of the impressions gained by the general public, as a result of all the hoohah, is that the country is divided up geographically, just like the federal states, and there's a kingpin for each section. This thinking makes it all easier to grasp, but it is also very misleading. What really happens is that there are a number of such kingpins in any given territory. Each has his own speciality, and care is taken to ensure that their interests do not conflict.

They operate over the same area, moving around each other, and concentrating on their own affairs. In a sense they are not unlike the various flavors in a complicated cooking recipe. Each makes its own distinctive contribution to the whole.

In a small town you may still come across the old-fashioned boss of bosses, an individual who really does have tentacles reaching into every part of the community's life. But in a large and wealthy community, it was recognised long ago that such a man was redundant. The whole structure would be too unwieldly to handle, too diverse to control. Once you start to lose control you have trouble, and trouble is something nobody needs or wants.

Communities don't come any lusher or richer than my particular part of Southern California. I knew there would be a boss in every field it was possible to name. Olive oil, vegetables, prostitution, gambling, the list is endless. There would be probably twenty or so men of real prominence in the criminal fraternity, and I had no idea which of them was the one who had hired me. That was why I needed to get access to Shad Steiner's files. He would be in there someplace, and all I had to do was search.

After about thirty minutes, I found him. There was no mistaking that face, and particularly the eyes. His name was Harrison Page, and he was third generation Greek. The Harrison came from Aristide, and the Page started out as something I couldn't even pronounce. I'd had him pegged as Italian, but that was probably because of my own preconditioning. There has been so much mythology about the Sicilian stranglehold on crime, that people conveniently forget the vast contribution made by other ethnic groups. Today's organisation bears no comparison with the position of fifty or even forty years ago. Today as in any legitimate structure, the best jobs go to the best people, give or take the odd blood relative.

Harrison Page was forty-six years old, and he'd been married to the same woman since he was seventeen. They had seven children, and the two eldest were already working for their father. Page's special interest was wine, and that told me something about him. For a Greek to achieve prominence in the wine trade, in a part of the world where the farmers and distribution people were predominantly Italian, meant that he was a man of special talents. It did nothing to assist my peace of mind.

I looked at some pictures of people associated with him, hoping to spot my two escorts, but I couldn't be sure of anything. Those big dark glasses made effective masks.

While I had the opportunity, I tried to find out more about the Halsettis, but there was very little about them. It was only to be expected. The Globe was concentrating chiefly on its own circulation area, and the Halsettis operated four hundred miles away. On top of which, they weren't even of much importance in their own city.

I left the building without reporting back to Steiner. He would only ask questions, and he was very good at it. On the whole I preferred to have him think. I didn't know how to behave, rather than that I was holding out on him.

'Hey.'

A man's voice came from the side of the building, and a figure detached itself from the gloom, walking towards me.

'You got no right to park here,' he said. 'All these slots is like reserved.'

I put on my disarming smile, doubtful whether he could see it in the half-light.

'It's O.K.,' I assured him. 'I just paid a quick call on Shad Steiner.'

He was up close now.

'Really?' he replied. 'And how is old Shad?'

There was metal in his hand and it was pointing in the general area of my middle. The conversation had taken a turn for the worse.

'He's fine. Would that be a gun?'

'It would,' he confirmed. 'You wanta hear it go off?'

'No,' I assured him hastily. 'I'll take your word for it. Am I being stuck up?'

When he answered, his voice was aggrieved.

'Do I look like one of those no-hopers?

Hah, this is no stick-up. The piece is just like to kill you with if you make any trouble.'

That might have been reassuring to my new friend, but it did nothing for me.

'I don't like trouble,' I retorted quickly. 'What happens now?'

'Now we take a walk around the corner. Nice and easy. We're all going to have a nice talk.'

All. That didn't sound very promising either. That meant he wasn't alone. He wasn't close enough for me to try for the gun, maintaining a steady four foot gap between us. I was going to have to play along. His whole demeanour told me he was no stranger to the gun in his hand.

'That corner there?'

'You got it. Get moving.'

I walked reluctantly ahead of him, to where a car sat without lights. It seemed to be my day for dark limousines. A door swung open as we approached. I looked at my captor, and he nodded me inside, climbing in after me. He waved me away with the gun until I was wedged up in the far corner, by the other door. There was

61

no inside handle. There never is.

'Did you frisk him?'

The question came from in front. Now that my eyes were adjusting to the interior gloom I could make out a second man, half-turned towards me. He had a gun too.

'Nah,' denied the parking attendant. 'That woulda give him a chance to jump me. It don't matter if he's carrying. His coat is buttoned. By the time he gets to the iron, he'll be wearing a few more buttonholes.'

All of which made nice cold common sense, but I found it very onesided.

'So what happens now?' I queried.

'Now we talk,' said Front-Seat. 'You tell us what we want to know, and who can tell? Maybe you just walk away.'

'That is if you talk straight,' said Back-Seat. 'You start giving us a lot of double-chatter, and things won't be so nice.'

'What'll we talk about?'

I tried to keep my voice calm, but I didn't like the set-up at all. These people were too relaxed to suit me. In my business, you get to know when guys are just making noises. Half the time they're just as nervous as the man they're trying to throw a scare into. These two were not in that category. They meant what they said. If they got the right answers, they would let me go. If not, I wouldn't be going anywhere, and they wouldn't even raise their voices when they saw me off.

'Let's talk about Benny Hall,' suggested Back-Seat. 'What do you know about him?'

'Just that he's dead,' I replied evenly. 'I never heard of the man. Not before today.'

'Kinda funny, you finding him that way. You being such a big detective and everything.'

I wondered how many more times I was going to have to go through the same routine. Well, practise makes perfect, they say. I went into my act again, about Horace Winters, and the man kneeling beside the body. The whole spiel. From time to time they would interrupt with supplementary questions, in an attempt to trip me up. But you can't do that with a man who's only reciting the facts.

'Is this the way you told it to the coppers?' demanded Front-Seat.

'It's practically word for word.'

Back-Seat tutted impatiently.

'Seems funny to me,' he muttered. 'Seems to me the law woulda held you over, like being a material witness and all.'

He was making a point for me, and I grabbed at it.

'Right,' I nodded. 'And that's exactly what would have happened, if they thought I wasn't telling all I knew. The way things were, they were satisfied they had it all. And besides, they know me.'

'Huh? What's that supposed to mean?'

This from the front of the car.

'It means,' I explained, 'that I've been operating in this city a long time. The police don't exactly love me, but they do know me. They know how I work, they know my style. Like I said, they were satisfied.'

'You coulda been playing it smart,' objected Back-Seat. 'You coulda give it to

64

Benny yourself, then just stayed around, acting dumb.'

'Oh sure,' I scoffed, with returning confidence. 'And where did I put the gun? I don't know how many thirty-twos you swallowed lately, but believe me, they give you lumps in the throat.'

'There coulda been another guy with you,' insisted Back-Seat doggedly. 'You coulda slipped him the artillery.'

'I don't work with other people,' I stated. 'And you can ask anyone in this town. I'm just a man who was out looking for another man, and happened along when Benny paid his dues.'

There was silence for a while, as they thought about it. Then Front-Seat said

'What were you doing at the newspaper?'

'Went to see the night editor. He's an old friend of mine. I call in there now and then, to see what's going on around the city. It's useful in my line of work. Sometimes I can get a few hours start on a lead.'

'You was in there a long time,' grunted Back-Seat suspiciously.

'Well,' I said, with what I hoped was

disarming frankness, 'if you must know, it isn't only the night editor I call on. There's a certain lady reporter in there, she's kind of like an old friend, too. Only not too old, if you follow me.'

They liked it better. The atmosphere relaxed noticeably.

'How about that?' chuckled Front-Seat. 'There's us sitting out here, and there's him in there screwing. It don't seem fair.'

'Right,' agreed Back-Seat easily. But he never eased his hold on the gun.

'Look,' I ventured, 'I'm not a man who pokes a nose in where it isn't wanted, but what is it with this Benny Hall thing? I mean, was he somebody important, or what?'

The two men looked at each other, and seemed to reach some kind of agreement.

'Let's put it this way,' said Front-Seat slowly. 'Benny wasn't nobody special. Not himself. But he had important connections. These important connections don't like it when one of their crew gets bumped off. They have to do something about it.'

'If they don't,' supplemented his

partner, 'then maybe the idea gets around that things ain't what they were. Next thing you know, every clown with his own piece starts setting himself up in business, and then what do you have?'

'Uproar,' continued the other. 'Uproar is what you have, and that's what we can't stand for. All over this town, every town, people are waiting. They're waiting to see what's going to be done about Benny.'

'And we are here to do it,' was the final pronouncement. 'Put this down as one of your lucky nights, Preston. If we didn't believe you, you was dead five minutes ago.'

I swallowed. The matter-of-factness of his tone carried more cold menace than any shouted threats. What he had said was no more than the plain truth.

'What happens now? Do I go?'

Again, there was that unspoken exchange between them.

'I guess so,' agreed Front-Seat finally. 'We'll be around till this thing gets cleared up. Don't let us hear bad things about you, Preston. If you been pitching us a yarn, we'll be looking for you.'

'Yeah. And we know where to find you,'

agreed his stable-mate.

He eased himself backwards out of the car, waggling the gun for me to do the same. When I was standing outside, he said 'Just for interest, are you carrying?'

I shook my head.

'No. I don't tote those things unless I'm on business. Besides, the lady reporter doesn't like guns. They make her nervous.'

He accepted this morsel with lascivious interest.

'That a fact? I knew this dame once, she was just the opposite. What she used to do was, she used to — '

He dropped his voice, as though we were in a crowded bar. That would have been a more suitable venue for the tale he was telling. After that, we exchanged a few winks and smiles, and I went away, steeling myself not to run.

Back in my own car, I wiped a handkerchief across my brow. It had not been a good day. I seemed to spend most of my time on the wrong end of conversations with people who would kill me at the drop of a hat. That is bad enough when I know what it's all about.

When I'm involved. It's very much worse when I really am as innocent as I claimed to be.

One thing seemed clear. Harrison Page wanted the Benny Hill case cleared up so that he could demonstrate to the boys from up-state that he ran a clean operation. My latest tormentors were not working for Page. They were not known to me as local people. That made it a fair assumption that the San Francisco crowd had sent in their own unit. Either that, or the Halsetti familiy had decided not to wait around while the big wheels went into operation. They could have sent two of their own guns in on a wild-cat job, and to hell with the organisation.

All kinds of assumptions were available, but one thing was clear, and becoming clearer by the minute.

This was no pipe and slippers case. This wasn't the one where a man sat around examining theories and motivations at leisure. It was a situation calling for action, the faster and more explosive the better.

This was one for the streets.

4

The late Beniamino Halsetti had been living at the Almira Apartments, which is what the city developers would class as a lower middle income group rented accommodation unit. Other people would call it a rather run-down apartment building, just this side of respectable. The rooms were functional, the services minimal, and the clientele transitional. It was the kind of place where a man could stay a few days on his way through, a few weeks on his way down. A place of drawn curtains, and not much sign of life.

I double checked that all the car-doors were locked before I left it. There wasn't any way to lock up the wheels.

The revolving glass doors to the building seemed to have met with some kind of accident. They hung at a jaunty angle which announced clearly they were temporarily retired from the revolving business. I tried the small service door at the side and found it open. In the tiny hallway, a flap counter suggested that at one time in its career, the Almira had boasted some kind of reception service. Those days were long gone, and the area was stacked with old cartons and dusty newspapers. There was a badly-lettered sign on the wall which stated 'No Cooking in the Rooms', but the grease-laden air indicated that some of the residents couldn't read. A door beside the reception/garbage area bore the legend 'MAN GER'. I thought it was unlikely anyone kept horses in there. It was more feasible that the letter 'A' had dropped out of manager.

There were two choices open to me. I could go it alone, and take my little peek at Benny's living quarters, running the risk of being tagged as an intruder. Or, I could dig out the building manager, and publicise my presence.

I banged on the door. From inside, I could hear the teevee, turned up to full throttle. I banged again, harder. The door half-opened, and a man inspected me. He was a big fleshy man, wearing a lumber-jack shirt and worn jeans. A thin line of hair ran around the lower half of his head, while the upper half shone like a billiard ball in the light from behind him.

'We're full up,' he advised me, and began to close the door.

I stuck my foot in it.

'Not quite,' I contradicted. 'One of your tenants got himself bumped off today. That gives you one vacancy.'

'No it don't, smart-ass,' he retorted smugly. 'Guy was paid up to the end of the month. Shift the foot.'

'In a minute. I'd like to see the apartment. Here's my identification.'

I held out a ten-dollar bill.

He looked at the money with quick interest, then back at me.

'Whaffer?' he demanded. 'There's nothing up there. Cops went through it like a suction pump.'

'I'd like to see for myself,' I insisted. 'Besides, what do you care? My papers are in order.'

I rustled the banknote. He was weakening.

'I don't know,' he muttered. 'Maybe I

72

could get in some kind of trouble.'

'For showing me an empty room?' I scoffed. 'Besides, who's going to know? You're not going to tell anybody, and neither am I.'

He came out nodding.

'Yeah, I guess so. But I come with you.'

'Glad of the company,' I assured him.

We went up in a wheezy elevator. There was no conversation. At seven, we got out and I followed him to 712. He unlocked the door, and we went in. The apartment consisted of two rooms. One was for sitting in, the other a bedroom. It was a functional place, with little to stamp the identity or interests of the occupant. At the end of the month, the manager would sweep around lightly, and the next tenant would move in, to make the same nil impact. I looked in the wardrobe. Benny Hall was not a great dresser, that much was clear. One item seemed out of place. It was a woolly red and blue hat, with a white bobble on the top. I lifted it down, staring at it.

'Did you ever see him wear this thing?' I queried.

'Nah,' he denied. 'That would be the kid's.'

Any boredom I might have been feeling vanished instantly.

'What kid are we talking about?' I asked softly.

'Dinnya know? There was this kid with him. His daughter.'

No. I didn't know. And now I wanted to know more.

'What sort of age would she be?'

He made a face, and shrugged.

'I don't know about kids. These days, they could be any age. Twelve maybe, fourteen. Who knows?'

'Did you see her, talk to her?'

The bald head revolved a negative.

'Nah. I seen her a couple of times, coming and going. Nice kid, you know, like fresh-looking.'

'Well, did she go to school around here, or what?'

But he'd had enough of me and my questions.

'Look, I don't do social work, I rent apartments. Maybe she went to school, I wouldn't know. Listen, I been talking to cops half the day and I couldn't tell them anything either. Schools keep records, don't they? Ask around.'

He wasn't holding out on me. He really didn't know. I replaced the hat where it belonged.

'Where's the girl now? Did the police get somebody to look after her?'

'She ain't been back. Not that I know of. Maybe she got scared and ran off.'

'Why would she do that?'

Now he looked pained.

'Aw, come on. Ain't you forgetting something? Ain't you forgetting some-body put a coupla slugs in her daddy? That is liable to upset a child, wouldn't you say?'

That hadn't been what I meant. What I meant was, how was she to know about her father's murder? Had she been there when it happened? Did she see it on the teevee news, and if she did, where was she when she saw it, and who was she with at the time? And another thing — Well, a hundred other things, but it was no use asking the building manager about any of it.

'Did you catch her name?'

'Angie. Name was Angie.'

I waved a hand around the room.

'She must have had some other clothes, personal items. There's nothing here.'

'Cops took it all. They said the city would have to look after her until they could trace the rest of the family.'

'But they would have to find her first,' I objected.

'Right,' he agreed. 'You about through here?'

'Give me another couple of minutes.'

I prowled around, without much hope. One thing you would have to say about the Monkton City P.D., they were thorough. They had been through this place with care, and I wasn't going to come up with the missing jewels, no matter how hard I looked. The waste basket is usually a productive area, but even that told me nothing. There was some orange peel, half a torn wrapper from a hi-speed film, and two empty cigaret packs. They were different brands. One was strong tobacco, and the other a light menthol product where tobacco was in the minority.

I looked up from my kneeling position.

'It's a cinch these two brands weren't smoked by the same person,' I pointed out. 'Did little Angie smoke?'

His features became bland.

'Not in front of me,' he intoned carefully. 'That would be against the law, wouldn't it?'

I grinned. The affront in his tone, at the suggestion that anyone in the vicinity of the Almira Apartments should in any way offend against the law, struck me as comical. Especially a serious crime like under-age smoking.

'Yes, I imagine it would,' I agreed. 'But so is murder.'

There was stuff in the bathroom that confirmed the presence of a young female. Hand cream, talcum powder, and so forth. I would have given a lot for five minutes' conversation with the owner.

'Well, there's nothing here,' I decided.

'You ain't very thorough are you?' accused my escort. 'Cops was hours going through this place.'

'That's why I'm not wasting any more

of my time,' I replied. 'Those guys are good. Anything here worth finding, they found it. All they leave the rest of us is orange peel.'

We didn't talk on the way down, each busy with his own thoughts.

Outside his apartment I said

'Well, thanks for your trouble. It was a waste of time, just like you said.'

He nodded with satisfaction.

'Told you it would be.'

He went back inside, and I walked towards the street door. As his door closed, I went back on my steps, and into the reception desk recess. Making a cup of my hands, I pressed them against the wall adjoining the manager's apartment. It wasn't a very effective sound-box, but I could hear the television, still blaring away. Suddenly it ceased, and all was quiet. I tried to screw my hands into the plaster in an attempt to improve the volume. After a few seconds, I picked up a low mutter from the adjacent room. Either there was someone else in with the manager or he was talking on the telephone. I couldn't pick up any words, only the distant voice-hum. But there was no mistaking the pinging sound when the receiver went back into place. Picking my way through the junk, I went and banged on his door again.

This time it opened at once, and his recognition carried no pleasure.

'You forget something?' he demanded.

'Just one little thing,' I admitted easily. 'I forgot to ask you who paid you to tip them off if anyone came around asking questions.'

Guilt stood out from every sweat-bead on his forehead.

'I don't know what you're talking about,' he blustered. 'Shove off.'

'Now, now,' I pushed hard against the door, hitting him on the shoulder. It took him off balance long enough for me to step inside. I closed the door behind me. 'Might as well be private. Never know who might be listening out in the hallway.'

'We got nothing to talk about,' he said uneasily. 'Better get out of here, before I turn nasty.'

'Oh tut tut,' I tut-tutted. 'Please don't

get rough with me. I couldn't stand it. I mean, just look at all that muscle round your middle.'

I jabbed at him from about six inches. It wasn't a vicious blow, but my hand disappeared up to the wrist in lard. He gave a great whooshing sound, and staggered away, folding up. The heavy jowls took on a light green tinge.

'Now then,' I continued conversationally, 'these friends of yours. Who are they?'

'I don't know what — all right, all right.'

His denial died on his lips, as I took a half-pace forwards, and he collapsed into a chair.

'Do you know you can kill a man like that?' he demanded petulantly. 'Man my age, little bit out of condition, you can cause all kinds of ruptures and internal bleeding. Did you know that? There was this article about it the other day.'

'You didn't read it properly,' I told him lightly. 'Before you can do any of that kind of damage you have to work your way through all the fat. You have fat we

80

didn't even start on yet. Now then, what about these contacts of yours? And I don't have all night to listen to fairy tales.'

He pressed a hand against his stomach, still wincing.

'I don't know,' he whimpered, half to himself. 'There was this guy, he seemed real mean to me.'

It seemed that we might be making some progress.

'But he's not here,' I pointed out cheerfully. 'I am, and I can get pretty mean too. You want another demonstration?'

I half-raised my hand, and he pulled himself deeper into the chair.

'No, no, I'll tell you. This guy come around, it would be two o'clock, two-thirty. He gave me twenty five dollars. All I had to do was tell him anything that happened that had any connection with the murder.'

'What was his name?'

'He didn't tell me — no wait, godammit, he didn't tell me. All he did was, he give me this number. Said I was to call if anything broke.'

I began to believe him.

'Could have been a newspaper man,' I suggested.

He looked aggrieved.

'Certainly not. This was a trouble man. Believe me, I've been around long enough to know one of those people when I see one.'

'All right. Give me the number.'

The bald head shook.

'I can't do that. No telling what this guy might do to me.'

'Yes, you can,' I contradicted. 'Because there's also no telling what I might do to you. And I'm here. That's the difference. Don't look so worried. If it'll make you feel any better, I'll promise you something. He'll never know I got the number from you.'

Something that might have been the beginning of hope began to spread across his unhappy features.

'You mean it?'

'Why not? I've got nothing against you. Why would I want to cause you any grief? Just give me the number, and I'll go away. It'll be strictly between you and me.'

'It's written down over there,' he

waved. 'Next to the phone.'

I copied the number down. He watched anxiously, hoping soon to be rid of me.

'One last thing. How many times have you called him so far?'

His eyes narrowed, as he cogitated the pros and cons of holding out on me. Then he shrugged.

'What's the diff? I called him once. Just the one time.'

'What did you have to report?' I demanded.

He rolled his eyes in misery.

'Listen, I could get my head busted,' he whined.

'Right,' I agreed. 'Any time in the next two minutes, if you don't start giving out. About the report you made.'

'It was nothing, really. Just a coupla guys come around here, asking questions. They said they were Hall's relatives, but I don't know.'

'Did they go up to the apartment?'

He contrived a small grin.

'They wanted to. There was still a cop up there. When I told them that, they got kinda jumpy and took off.'

'What did they look like?'

From the clumsy phrases, plus a couple of promptings from me, I was able to make it a reasonable assumption that the callers had been my friends of the front and rear seats.

'If those people are who I think they might be, let me give you a little advice. If they come back again, don't give them any fancy chatter. Just do it their way, and you'll be O.K. Start with the double talk and you'll regret it. Not everybody is as gentle as me.'

That produced a sound best described as a half-snort.

'Now then, tell me about the other report,' I suggested.

'What other one,' he queried, wide-eyed. 'There wasn't no other one. Just the one I'm telling you about.'

I wagged a finger.

'You're going to have to do something about that memory. The other report was about me. You just finished making it.'

'Oh, that,' he nodded. 'Yeah, well there wasn't much to tell.'

'Did you tell him who I was?'

He was all innocence now.

'No. Honest, I wouldn't do that. I just said you was a guy who — '

The words trickled away into silence, as he realised what he was saying. The look on my face might also have had something to do with it. The manager had made a mistake. He shouldn't have said he concealed my identity. He should have said he didn't know who I was.

If he'd been nervous before, he was terrified now. His face was working, and breath was coming out of him in short jerky gasps.

'So you know who I am.'

I made it a soft, dangerous kind of statement.

'Look Mr. Preston, you don't have to worry about me. I'm not mixed up in this. I don't even know what's going on. I'm only what you see, just the manager, for chrissakes.'

'Did the two men ask about me?'

He was anxious to answer now, anxious to demonstrate his all-round good-guyness.

'Yeah. They wanted to know if you ever

85

come here, if I ever seen you with Hall. Stuff like that.'

'And what'd you tell 'em?'

'What could I tell 'em? I said I never heard of you before today. Not till I seen you on the tee vee. I told the cops the same thing.'

The conversation was broadening.

'Oh, so the police asked about me too? You forgot to mention that before.'

Light bounced from his head like a reflector as it moved up and down.

'Just slipped my mind, is all. They wanted to know if I knew you. They had your picture with them.'

I had to hand it to Schultz. He was thorough. He said he believed my story. He turned me loose. Then he sent out guys with pictures. It didn't say much for the man's trustful nature. I decided the manager was about dry. On information, that is. Everything else about him was soaked in sweated fear.

'You look like you need a drink. Any booze around? We'll all have one.'

The change of subject was very much to his liking.

86

'There's rye. In that cupboard there.'

I took it out, along with two glasses. I put four fingers in one, and just wet the bottom of the other. Handing him the big dose, I said

'Well, here's to a long life.'

He grabbed at the liquor and slopped it down gratefully.

'My, my, you were thirsty,' I chided. 'Why didn't you say so?'

I refilled his glass, almost to the brim. He eyed it unhappily.

'I don't usually drink so fast,' he demurred.

'A man should drink according to the company. You're in fast company, my friend. You wouldn't want to insult me by not drinking with me?'

'Oh no, no.'

He dipped his face in the tumbler again, but could only manage half the contents. I put another quarter inch in my own glass.

'We were drinking to a long life,' I reminded him. 'Or maybe that doesn't interest you?'

He nodded feverishly, and took another pull at the rye.

'That's better,' I filled him up again. 'Tell you what, let's kill this, and I'll go get us some more. We'll make it a party.'

His eyes were becoming bleary now, as the alcohol began to take hold.

'I can't figure you out,' he told me confidentially.

'In what way?'

'Well, you know.' He heaved his shoulders around in a gesture of puzzlement. 'One minute you're laying into a man, next thing I know we're drinking like it's a reunion or something.'

'That's me,' I agreed cheerfully. 'Unpredictable. Well, I'm about ready for some more, and I'm sure you are too. We'll drink to the memory of old Benny Hall.'

'Who?'

'Hall,' I repeated. 'The man upstairs. He got murdered today. We ought to show a little respect. Up on your feet.'

He made it at the second attempt, and was far from steady on his pins. I had to hold his drinking hand steady as I poured out another helping.

'Benny was a Balinese, did you know that?'

'Ba Bali- what?'

'A Balinese. They have this firewater dance they always do at funerals. What you do is, you take a drink, then you dance a bit, then you take another drink, then you dance some more. All the men in the village have to take part, it's compulsory. You ready?'

A foolish grin occupied the lower half of his face.

'Dance? Me? I ain't danced in twenty years.'

'You'll dance now. Or would you rather insult the dead?'

I put some edge into my tone, and he looked horrified.

'No, no,' he denied. 'I guess I can remember.'

'First, you drink.'

Maybe the Balinese do have a firewater dance for all I know. If not, they ought to introduce it right away. It would be worth it, to see the kind of cavorting produced by the building manager of the Almira Apartments. Five minutes of the drinking, panting and shuffling, and he was a gone goose.

'You gonna call somebody?'

He was peering across the room, to where I was pulling the telephone plug out of the wall socket.

'Firewater god,' I assured him. 'Have to call him up, make sure he's pleased with the ceremony. He won't like it if you're not drinking.'

'Oh sure,' he'd dispensed with the glass, and was now clutching the fifth as he pranced around. There was about an inch left in the bottom.

He was in no state to make any telephone calls, but the phone works both ways. There was nothing to stop him from answering if it rang.

'Finish that up,' I ordered. 'I'll go get us some more.'

The bottle tilted up to his face and some of the rye went down his mouth. The rest ran all over his chin.

'You'll be right back, huh? Where you taking the phone?'

I shook my head pityingly.

'I have to have it with me. Suppose somebody calls me while I'm out? I have to be able to answer, right?'

He seemed to understand that. He stood in the centre of the room, blinking like a worried owl and swaying from side to side. I gave him five minutes to blackout point, ten at the outside.

Nodding encouragement, I left the apartment with the telephone in one hand. Outside, I dropped it into one of the cartons on the reception counter. The manager was going to need a long undisturbed sleep, and we couldn't have the telephone bothering him.

The evening heat was oppressive when I got back to the car. Inside, I sat for a few moments, reviewing the situation. Whatever else this case might turn out to be, it certainly wasn't one of those deals where a man could waste a month of his life chasing one tiny lead. It was more like some kind of brass band parade, with hoodlums of various factions and teams of police officers chasing all over the city, upsetting people. Well, upsetting me, anyway. And how about the Schultz, waving my picture around that way? Next thing you knew, I would be appearing on one of those have-you-seen-this-man posters.

It's a very disturbing thing, for a man not to feel trusted, and right in my own town, too. Particularly when he's working for a public figure like Mr. Harrison Page, the distinguished racketeer.

Offhand, I couldn't think of one redeeming feature about this case. I didn't like what I was doing, the people I was doing it for, or what everybody seemed anxious to do to me.

At that moment there were two unexplored avenues, both new. One was the little girl, Angie Hall. Her father had been murdered just a few hours earlier, and maybe she'd even been a witness. The poor kid was probably holed up somewhere, unhappy and frightened, but I wouldn't know how to start looking for her, certainly not at ten o'clock at night. With luck, the police would have traced her, and if they had, I was worrying about nothing. She'd be warm and safe wherever they put her, and I could do nothing about her personal misery.

The other lead was different.

A telephone number meant an address. An address meant a name and a face. The face was one I wanted to see. He'd thrown a scare into my late drinking partner and that would have to be looked into.

One thing about us Balinese firewater dancers, we stick together.

5

It took a few minutes of chatter before I
could locate someone on the night shift at
the telephone company who knew me.
After that, it was less than a minute
before I had a title and an address to go
with the phone number. The title was
impressive. Still-Life Portraits Inc., the
address less so. That was a number on
Conquest Street, which is a big minus to
any business concern.

Every city has a Conquest Street,
although they don't always give it such a
fancy title. Monkton was originally a
Spanish outpost, complete with mission
and stone-built fort. Those old-time
explorers left their mark in many ways,
and there are those who will tell you that
Conquest Street stands on the site of the
old camp road. They will tell you that the
name itself, Conquest, is a deterioration
of the original Spanish, which was
Conquistadores. But then, people will tell

you anything. I don't have any Spanish blood, but I have Spanish friends, and I wouldn't want to think their claims to immortality had to rest in a rathole like Conquest Street.

Not that it's all rathole. It starts off the corner of Fourth, in the heart of the business section, which is as legitimate as you can get. There is even a real live theater there. Older people will know what I mean by live theater. It is a place where actors put on plays, and they have to learn the words off by heart, and do everything for themselves. They do it in front of real people, who pay money to watch them. They do the whole thing right through, from beginning to end, with no retakes, no close-ups, and no studio applause. It's a very out-of-date art form, and naturally it only lasted a few thousand years. The Greeks started it, but what did they know? They didn't even have intercontinental ballistic missiles.

Anyway, there's this legit theater, then one or two business houses. There's even a money mart, where they will exchange your foreign currency at almost the legal market rate. Then things change, slowly at first. Almost legal becomes not quite legal, which becomes barely legal and so forth. By the time you get halfway down the street it is downright scarey. A raucous half-world of pin-ball parlors, would-be 'atmosphere' cellars, blue movies and bluer conversation. Strip joints and clip joints, guys wearing paint and dames wearing moustaches. A place of hoarse invitations to step right in. They say there's a fortune waiting for the man who can come up with a new decadent diversion, something that isn't already catered to a hundred times over. But there's a lot of ingenuity been poured into the decadence business across the years. Now that I think of it, didn't the Greeks start that, too?

I drove slowly down the brightly lit street, the jangle of a hundred canned music places beating into the car. Still-Life Portraits Inc. was a narrow fronted two-story building, wedged in between a mission hall and a chili parlor. Pulling into the kerb, I looked around until I spotted them. A gang of youths, clustered outside a bookie joint, were just what I needed. Some white, some black, some in-between, these were the liege lords of that particular section of real estate. It was their turf, and they would defend it against all comers, with knife, club or whatever came to hand. Their great strength was also their weakness, because it could be turned against them. Their own code forbade them to desert their turf, and that meant they could always be found there.

I got out of the car and locked it up. They watched me covertly. Two of them were cavorting around to a portable radio, and all pretended to be looking the other way as I approached. One of them was slightly apart from the rest. He was tall and husky-looking, with a beaver skin hat, and a silver medallion that dangled against his open chest. Thick white suspenders were clamped onto greasy jeans which tailed away inside scuffed cowboy boots.

'You the chief of this clan?'

It was as though I didn't exist. He remained, head bowed, staring at his feet.

From my right, somebody gave a low dog howl.

'Are you deaf, greaseball?'

Slowly his head came upright, and pale eyes glittered from the dank hair flopping around his face.

'You talking to me?'

'Only if you're the head man.'

'What is this, a raid?'

He spoke with a slight wisp, and this witticism brought laughs and catcalls from his watching supporters.

'Kind of,' I returned. 'Got a job for you.'

'A job?' He rolled his eyes, and looked at the others. 'Hey, this man brings us employment. He gonna raise us from this here environment, and show us the true path. We gonna be wage-earners for the honkeys. What's it gonna be, man? Load that barge, tote that bale? Tell you what, I'll screw your mother for a nickel.'

'Sure you will,' I replied easily. Pulling out the thirty eight, I shoved him hard against the wall, ramming the automatic against his throat. There was a gasp from his followers, and now the atmosphere was electric. 'I wouldn't want to work you too hard. See that car over there? That's my car. It goes along with me, and I goes along with this. You and these horse-droppings are going to keep an eye on it. Anything happens to it, I am going to blow you away. You have the picture?'

He wasn't too scared. This was a business conversation, gun or no. He probably didn't doubt that I would use it, but first I would have to have a reason.

'Oh sir,' he entreated, 'please do not shoot me. You will make holes in my fine young body. What is this about the car?'

'It stops where it is,' I explained. 'It stops the way it is, wheels and all. Anything happens to it, I blame you.'

He rolled his eyes in mock fear.

'Dis a low low priority neighborhood, mister man. All kinds of people down here. I even hear there is a criminal element. Spose some of dis yere criminal element makes a personal appearance? No telling what might happen.'

'No problem,' I assured him. 'I blame you. If lightning strikes, I blame you. No matter what, I blame you. Am I coming through?'

His eyes narrowed now, as he squinted down at the piece. I gave it an extra grind against his throat, making him wince.

'You display a certain harshness of spirit, sir. There's a raw element in your disposition which is very unappealing. Don't you read the social welfare programme? Don't you know we are the deprived, the hopeless ones? You have a responsibility of conscience to such as us. And what, pray, is there in it?'

With my free hand I gave him a torn twenty dollar note.

'When I come back, you get the other half.'

He took the bill, his followers watching every move.

'Maybe,' he shrugged. 'Depends how long you're gonna be. We got a lot of big deals coming up. Heavy schedule, you know?'

I was satisfied.

'Could be five minutes. Could be an hour, I don't know. What's it to you? You have a whole new social position. You are now a forty grand a year man.'

'Yeah? How'd I get to be one of those, mister sir?'

I stepped away from him.

'Let's say it takes me an hour. You collect twenty. If you do that forty hours a week, that's eight hundred. Eight hundred a week is forty grand per. You ought to move out this neighbourhood, man in your position.' He put his right hand across his heart.

'The land of opportunity. Mama was right.'

'Just watch the car.'

I kept them all in view as I walked across the street. There were no lights coming from inside Still-Life Portraits Inc. but sufficient of the street lighting spilled across the windows for me to check the display. It was the usual run of blushing brides, young guys in ill-fitting tuxes, kids standing beside bored-looking ponies. A card stuck in one corner announced that George Luckman was available to cover all social functions. The telephone number was the one I'd brought from the Almira Apartments. I tried the door, and it was securely bolted. It would have been an easy matter to find a telephone and call Mr. Luckman, but that would give him an edge. That would tell him there was somebody else taking a hand in the game, and I preferred him to learn that when I could see him.

Stepping around the side of the building I walked down a narrow alley, edging carefully past overspilling trash cans. There was another door at the far end. Checking continually over my shoulder, to ensure that the car-minders were not creeping up on me, I tried the door handle, without much hope. It swung open, with a creak that sounded like a gunshot in that still air. One last check around, and I stepped inside. Something was not right. The kind of man described by the manager at the Almira was not the kind to leave doors unlocked. I closed it behind me, and stood still, letting my eyes get accustomed to the gloom. I was in a kitchen, and one thing was sure. There was no woman around the house. The place was more like a pigsty, with piles of open cans and bottles and dirty dishes on all sides. Whatever else he might be, Luckman was not a retired restaurateur.

Another door stood open, leading into the rest of the premises, and I could see a faint glow of red light. My first reaction was fire, but I corrected it at once. No fire would produce a steady glow like that, certainly not in this rat trap. The place would go up like the Fourth of July. Keeping the thirty eight at the ready, I moved out into the passageway. There was a door to the left, which had to lead into the shop-front. It was closed, and I ignored it for now, moving towards that strange light, which I could now see came from a door at the further end.

Edging carefully along, I stuck my nose around and peered inside. I was looking into a photographer's dark room, and that was the reason for the red light. There were trays of chemicals, and strips of film dangling in all directions, and now I knew something was up. The photographer hasn't been born who will leave his darkroom door open, not even in an emergency.

Two choices were open. There was the door behind me, the one leading to the store, and there was a stairway. I selected the door, but it was locked, and that left only the stairs and whatever was to be found above. The treads were thickly carpeted, and I made no sound as I moved upward into darkness. At the top, I stood stockstill for a full minute, straining my ears. The only sound was from my own heart, doing its trip-hammer imitation. But there was a smell, a light, nostril-stinging smell that was only too familiar. Cordite. A gun had been fired up here, and recently. Guns meant people, and if there was someone else around, someone with a gun, I was at a big disadvantage. The someone else would know the layout of the premises, and I didn't. Feeling around the wall, I located a light switch. In one movement I pressed it down and dropped to the floor. Nobody shot at me, and there I was stretched out on inch-thick plum-colored carpet. Whoever designed the building had not been very imaginative. The layout was a replica of the lower floor, just three doors, and all of them closed. I would have to open each one, and in sequence, starting with the room above the darkroom. To do it any other way would leave unexplored territory behind me, territory that could be hiding an armed man. Turning the first handle, and keeping to the cover of the wall, I peeked inside.

I was staring into what I could only describe as a dressing room, as in theater, but this was no time for close inspection. The room was empty, and that was all I needed to know at that moment. The next door led into the large room above the showroom. I pushed the door wide, keeping my body clear of the lighted space. Nobody shot at me, but that didn't have to mean anything. Sliding a hand around, I found a switch and pressed it, flooding the room with light. Then I moved cautiously in, to find myself standing in what was clearly a film studio. An empty film studio.

The final door was the one above the kitchen, and I went into my elaborate routine again, beginning to feel slightly foolish. The smell was strong in there, and

I was no longer alone. Stretched out on the bed was the body of a man. He'd been shot three times in the chest, and the dark blood was beginning to coagulate on his floral pajamas. Whoever shot him was long gone, and I put away my own gun with relief. He was a heavy-faced, balding man of forty plus, and the way he was positioned suggested that he was either standing by the bed or sitting on it when the gun went off. George Luckman was about to cover his last social function, and it would be his own funeral.

I poked around the bedroom, learning nothing except that the tenant had some rather fancy tastes in decor. Mauve walls and pink lighting seemed an odd choice for a guy who lived by himself. One wall was filled entirely by a sliding door wardrobe, and that made interesting looking. The first third was full of men's suits, sports jackets, and the like. The remainder was a varied collection of female stuff, long evening gowns, hostess gowns and so forth. In a husband and wife setting it would have been quite understandable, but the bed now occupied by the deceased Luckman remained uncompromisingly single.

I went back into the big room, the studio, and made a closer inspection. It was an odd set-up for an outfit calling itself Still-Life Portraits Inc. Three heavy professional video cameras were positioned at various heights, and pointing towards a mock-up of a cell-interior. Or perhaps torture-chamber would be more accurate. Heavy-looking chains and leg-irons were attached to the wall, and a discarded black whip lay on the narrow cot. There were one or two other contraptions in evidence whose purpose I could only guess at, but it all added up to one thing. The Still-Life tag was for downstairs. Up here we had the mobile kind, and the end product would not be for all social occasions. This was a blue-movie set, and it didn't take a very smart detective to work that out. It would explain what all that female clothing was doing in the bedroom, and it explained the dressing room. I went back to that little room and did a proper search. There was a cupboard, full of black leather and rubber items, some of the uses being obvious, and others for locker-room speculation.

Another, smaller cupboard was locked. Usually I would have left it alone, but I don't usually find myself in quite those circumstances.

The wooden doors splintered with a loud crack as I levered them apart. I was looking at the stock room. The interior was piled high with video cassettes and the titles did not lead me to suppose they were destined for nursery television. 'Sex-fiend from Mars', 'Julia's Erotic Nights' and so forth sounded more like the raincoat circuit. At the end of each title was a number, and it seemed logical to assume that these would be in sequence of age. Unfortunately for my theory, the titles were filed in alphabet order. That meant I had to wade my way through, looking for the highest numbers. It was only a remote possibility, but it struck me that the latest products would show pictures of people who had most recently worked with Luckman. They may or may not know anything about his murder, but they ought to be in a position to throw more light on his recent activities than someone who worked with him in the past.

I came up with ninety seven and ninety eight. The titles were 'Under-Age Nympho' and 'Insatiable Irma', and they went into my coat pocket. Apart from the movies, George Luckman seemed to keep no records. There were no books, no diaries, nothing. Luckman was either the most distrustful man ever, or someone had cleaned the place out.

Back in the bedroom, I went through the pockets of his suit. A part-used check book told me he had an account with the Metropolitan Bank, and it told me something else. Luckman was one of those rare people who make a proper note in check-stubs. A man who went to that kind of detail was not a man to run his business with no records, which confirmed my earlier thinking that his files had been taken. I stuck the check book inside my jacket for later scrutiny, and stood in the middle of the room, trying not to look at the corpse.

There had to be something. A man can't just die like that, and leave no trace that he ever existed. What I lacked was time. When the police came, they would have all the time in the world. They would find the missing wallet, the key to the safe-deposit box or whatever. But they wouldn't be in my position. I was a man who made what they would call a burglarious entry onto premises where another man had managed to get himself shot to death. To describe me as a suspicious character would be to put a very kind interpretation on my role, and the longer I stayed around, the greater was my chance of being discovered.

Reluctantly I took a final look around. The walls told me nothing, just like the first time. There was one last thing to do. With a handkerchief I went around wiping at any surface I had touched. The police would have loved me for that, too. In removing my own fingerprints, I was at the same time wiping off everyone else's, with the possible inclusion of the man with the gun. But this is a help-yourself society, and the first person to be helped by one Preston M. is Preston M.

Switching off lights as I went, I made my way downstairs. The darkroom still glowed, and I wished I knew more about the art of photography. For all I knew, there could be a dozen postcard size pictures of the killer in one of those trays, but they would have to wait for the police. One thing I did know was that light could be fatal to the images, and I would do better to leave things alone.

Before stepping out into the dark alley, I took out the Police Special. I didn't want to walk into my new employees without adequate preparation. They weren't waiting for me, and when I reached the welcome half-light of the street, they were in exactly the same place as I had left them.

I walked to the car, and unlocked the door. They moved very fast across to me and grouped themselves around.

'Hey man, you wouldn't be going off and leaving us?'

The words were casual, almost negligent. I shook my head.

'Don't worry. I just didn't want to give you underprivileged citizens the width of the street. A man could get run over. This way is more cosy.'

The chieftain shook his head in mock wonderment.

'Must be a terrible burden, having to tote around such a suspicious nature. Where is the bread?'

Keeping the automatic in plain view, I held out the other half of the twenty. Long slender fingers snapped around it.

'That's for the car,' he acknowledged. 'Tell you what, Preston, for another ten we'll forget you was here.'

The incidental dropping of my name was a development I hadn't foreseen. I looked at them, each in turn.

'How do I know I can trust you?'

The leader shrugged.

'You got a choice? Anyhow we ain't exactly the cops' favourite people. Just spread the ten and we will blow the scene.'

As insurance, it was all I was going to get. I passed over another ten dollars, and he nodded to the group who began to melt away.

'Nice doing business with you, sir.'

'Just keep your end,' I said nastily. 'Or things won't be quite so nice.'

'Oh tut tut,' he mocked. 'You shouldn't frighten me that way.'

I left them there. The radio was playing again, and one or two of them had begun to dance on the sidewalk. It was as though they'd forgotten I ever existed.

For my sake, I hoped they had.

6

Another large item in this cash flow problem we were talking about is my home address. I have this fancy apartment in the Parkside Tower, and it is a very O.K. piece of real estate, carrying a very O.K. price tag. Years of shakedowns, one-room walk-ups and the like had taught me to appreciate a little comfort.

On a mileage basis, Parkside isn't so very far from Conquest Street, but by any other measurement they are light-years apart. I let myself in, switching on lights. A man didn't have to be a trained observer to spot the difference between my place and the joint recently occupied by the late George Luckman. I pushed the play button on the answering machine and went to pour myself a drink.

'Mr. Preston.'

I almost slopped my scotch, as a resonant voice boomed into the room.

The voice was accustomed to command-ing attention, and my attention was duly commanded.

'I am Gettysburg Andrews of Andrews, Clark and Andrews. I should like you to come to my office tomorrow morning at ten o'clock. You will find it in your best interests to do so.'

The voice ceased, as abruptly as it had begun. That was it. Crossing to the machine, I played it again. I knew two things about Mr. Gettysburg Andrews. In the first place, he was a man who didn't waste words, and in the second place I didn't like him. Not a word of explana-tion. Not so much as a 'please'. Just 'be there'. And I didn't care for that bit about my best interests, either. If he'd said 'profitable', if he'd mentioned work, it would have made all the difference. But he didn't. The man practically threatened me. My first reaction was that I wouldn't go, but that was pure pique. I was going, because my best interests are one subject which can always be certain to claim my attention.

There were no other messages, so I

sprawled in a chair, lit an Old Favorite, and pulled out George Luckman's check book. He had a neat hand, and there was no problem in deciphering his entries on the stubs. He'd only used four checks out of the book, and they were routine payments — no they weren't. There were two made out to the telephone company, and only three days apart. Why? The amounts were different, and that meant two different bills. Two different bills meant two different telephones. I'd only found one instrument at Still-Life Portraits Inc. Cursing myself for not having thought of it sooner, I dug out a directory and began to thumb through it.

Because of the state of the kitchen, and because I found him dead in the bedroom, I had assumed Luckman lived on the premises. It just goes to show a man can't afford to make too many assumptions in this business.

There were three Luckman G's in the directory. I punched the first number out. After four rings, a voice said

'Hallo?'

'Mr. Luckman?'

'Yeah. Who is this?'

'Name is Brown. I want to get some pictures of my new car — '

' — pictures?' he interrupted. 'What is this, some kind of gag?'

'You are Mr. Luckman, Mr. George Luckman?'

'No. Name is Gerald. There is no George here.'

He hung up before I had a chance to apologise. The second number produced a woman's voice.

'Is that Mr. George Luckman's home?' I queried.

I didn't need any more Gerald situations.

'Yes it is,' she confirmed. 'Who is this calling?'

'Name is Brown,' I told her. 'Is Mr. Luckman there please?'

'I'm afraid not,' she cooed. 'Is there anything I can do?'

The voice was low and pleasant, the kind they use on the commercials when they want you to smoke pipe tobacco.

'It's a business matter,' I explained. 'What time will he be home?'

She paused.

'Not tonight, I'm afraid. He just phoned a few moments ago. From San Diego. He's got held up down there, and he won't be back until tomorrow. It's such a pity, I have this lovely dinner all ready.'

A few moments ago. My George Luckman hadn't made any calls for hours.

'That's too bad,' I consoled. 'I'll call tomorrow then.'

'Wait a minute,' she said. 'You sound like a nice man. There's this lovely meal just going to waste here. Why don't you come around? Maybe I could help you with your business. I help George all the time.'

I'll bet, I reflected. She must be a real tower of strength to old George.

'Love to,' I apologised, 'but it's my grandmother's birthday party tonight.'

I left her with her lovely dinner, and tried the third number. There was no answer. The address was out on Pearl Valley, a twenty minute drive. It was ten thirty at night, and I had nothing else to do. Assuming I had the right address, I had a head start on the law. They wouldn't be at the house tonight, because they didn't know Luckman was dead. That was confidential between me and whoever killed him.

The thought that the killer could be out there did nothing for my peace of mind, but I knew I would have to take that chance. Swallowing the last of my drink, I checked the thirty eight and stuck it in my waistband. Then I left the apartment.

Pearl Valley doesn't produce any pearls unless you count the ones around the female inhabitants' necks. The Valley was named after the wife of one of the early pioneers. That lady trekked three thousand miles across the continent through dust-storms, deserts, Indian attacks, the whole caboodle. By all accounts she was the driving force behind the little waggon train, always cheerful, and reviving peoples' spirits when things seemed at their most helpless. What nobody knew was that she was a sick lady herself, and when they reached the valley, just a few miles short of their goal, she died. They buried her there, under a shady tree, and named the place after her.

She wouldn't recognise the place now, I thought, as I began the descent down the steep winding highway. People need housing, and housing doesn't go along with rolling lush meadows. But the planners had been kinder than usual, and the Pearl Valley development was not the eyesore that certain other places were.

The Luckman address was on a road called Chipmunk Drive. The chipmunks, if there had ever been any, were long gone from the neat, tree-lined bungalow pattern. There were no lights on when I drew up outside the house, and no cars parked close by. If the killer was inside, he'd either walked or come on a bicycle. Neither alternative seemed very likely. I had my fingers firmly crossed as I approached the house. After all, it was no more than surmise on my part that this place tied in with my Luckman. It isn't the most unusual name in the world, and if I had it wrong, I was about to commit a crime against some perfectly harmless citizen. No one would be interested in my motives, even if they believed them, least of all the police. In any event I could never explain to anyone the impetus provided by the suave Mr. Harrison Page, and the not-so-suave Halsetti soldiers.

A narrow pathway alongside the house led to the rear. Back there, I was out of sight of the road and the neighbouring houses. Even these days, despite all the warnings and the mass of security equipment on the market, its childishly easy to break into most places. I was soon standing inside the house, listening. Now I had two choices. I could either paddle around in the dark, wasting a lot of time and doing a search which would necessarily be less than thorough. Or I could put a bold face on it, switch on all the lights, and be out within minutes. I pulled every curtain I could find, and switched on the lights.

The place was orderly. Not regimental, there was the odd cushion out of place, but overall neat. The Luckman who lived here behaved very differently from the slob on Conquest Street. I moved from room to room, doing my act with the curtains and lights. A man lived here, and he lived alone. There was no mistaking the signs. There was a wooden desk with an old-fashioned roll top in the living area. The lock was Mickey Mouse standard and responded quickly to a knife-blade. Inside was welcome confirmation that I was in the right place. A small pile of video cassettes occupied one of the neat compartments, and a quick glance at the titles told me all I needed to know.

But it was in a drawer that I struck the mother lode. Old George really did go in for some still-life work, and there was a pile of glossy pictures to prove it. They were pictures of men and women, doing what men and women have been doing since time began, but with one difference. The female was the same in all the pictures, and she wasn't a woman at all. She was no more than a kid, maybe fourteen years old, and the camera had caught her expression clearly every time. There was loathing, repulsion and naked terror shining out from every frame, and it turned my stomach. There seemed to be five different men involved, and their sweating straining faces were repulsive to the eye.

The background was the same every time. It was the bedroom on Conquest Street where I'd left George Luckman's bullet-riddled body. Seeing those pictures made me glad he was dead. My only regret was that he hadn't suffered more. I leaned against the desk, thinking. Luckman had probably been up to his ears in blackmail. Any one of the men in those pictures could have killed him, and there was no telling how many others were involved. The blackmailer never knows when to call a halt, and the record shows that a desperate victim will kill, if that becomes his only recourse. This was no job for me. It would take organisation, and a pack of trained investigators to dig out all these people. They were probably ordinary citizens, and even the possession of photographs would make it no easy task to trace them all. No. I had no doubts in my mind. This was one for homicide. They had all the manpower, all the technical backup, and I would only delay things by latching on to the photographs.

I went through them again, reluctantly, staring at each man's face, and trying to burn it into my memory. Then I replaced them in the drawer. The rest of the place told me little, outside of the fact that George Luckman liked to live well. There was one decoration that jarred against the rest.

The pictures, ornaments, and so forth were mostly unexceptional. Good quality, middle of the road stuff for the most part. And yet, in front of a large picture window, and resting on a solid metal table, there was an ugly surrealist piece of sculpture. It consisted of lumps of rock, cubes and ovoids mostly, balanced every which way to form — what? There was no shape I could recognise, no hint as to what it represented. To me, it was just a pile of rocks. The originator would probably have some tale about it. It represented the Spirit of Man, or Space and Beyond, or some fanciful flight, but so far as I was concerned, it was just a mess. The fact that the whole thing was coated thickly in shiny black paint did nothing to improve it.

I wasted a full minute looking at it, before carrying on with the search. As I had expected, it was a waste of time. George Luckman was a careful man. He wasn't about to leave all his money hidden under a loose floorboard. The only valuables in the place, outside the ornaments, consisted of fourteen one-dollar bills and three nickels.

Finally, I gave it up, switched off all the lights, and left the house. Tomorrow the police would arrive, and the search would be on for the violators of that little girl. It couldn't be too soon for me. My natural instinct was to telephone head-quarters and get them started right away, but my equally natural instinct for self-preservation told me to keep out of it.

I had plenty to think about on the drive back into town.

★   ★   ★

The prowl-car picked me up soon after I got inside the city limits. I sat patiently

125

behind the wheel, hands in plain view. I had no desire to get all shot up by some novice out on his first patrol.

A helmeted, heavily-armed figure appeared.

'Your name Preston?' rasped a voice.

My surprise was not faked.

'Yes,' I confirmed. 'What's the beef?'

'No beef,' he grunted. 'Got a message for you. You're to go down-town. The Homicide people want to see you. Ask for Detective Sergeant Randall.'

'I'm on my way,' I assured him. 'I'll report in.'

He stood watching, as I rolled away from the kerb. Then, satisfied, he walked back to his waiting partner.

This new development was a puzzler. For one thing, why was Randall involving himself suddenly? Schultz was a good man, and it was his case. Departmental protocol would normally require that he be given a reasonable crack at it, before anyone else interfered. That was one thing. The other thing was, why had Randall put my name on the wires? Police radio traffic is heavy, and they have to have a reason to take up valuable air space. I didn't care to be a reason, certainly not a valuable reason.

One thing about going to police headquarters late at night, at least a man can find a room to park a car. There are just as many police around as at any other time, just as many offenders, but the lost-canary squad have retired for the night, and that leaves plenty of space.

The duty sergeant nodded to me, and jerked his head towards the stairs. I went up slowly to the third floor, knowing better than to trust myself inside their suicidal elevator. The murder squad occupies three rooms up there, and Randall shared an office with the Captain of Detectives. This is a fancy title, and that's all it is. The city administration are too tight-fisted to dole out a captain's pay, and so the post is occupied by a touchy, irritable Irishman by the name of John Rourke. I hoped Rourke would not be present. Randall is bad enough by himself. Randall and Rourke together are a fearful combination, especially when it's close to midnight.

I tapped lightly on the grime-encrusted

glass and stuck my head around the door. Rourke's desk was vacant, Randall's was not.

'Ah,' he greeted, 'you decided to surrender.'

I went in, closing the door behind me, and sat down. They have this special chair for visitors. One of the legs pokes up through the wooden seat, and after twenty minutes a man will confess to anything, just to get to a nice, comfortable cell.

'Just for the record,' I replied, 'I want it noted down that I came in here of my own free will, to see if I could be of any assistance.'

Randall gave me one of his ponderous nods. He is a large shambles of a man, sixteen stone plus, with a heavy-jowled face and sleepy eyes that look as if he's been three days without rest. He often wears this bemused expression when he's talking to people, as though he's having difficulty, not only in keeping awake but also understanding whatever is being said to him. Anybody who meets him for the first time when he's on duty sums him up quickly. He is a slow-moving, slow-thinking man, who must have made sergeant because he has political relatives. He's certainly nothing to worry about, either physically, or in the brain department. That is the conclusion usually arrived at, and if you doubt my word, all you have to do is take a ride out to the penitentiary, or even the county jail. Those places get a lot of their business from people who have summed up Randall in this way. They will tell you with astonishment that they still haven't figured how it was he took away the knife or the gun, how he managed to crack an unshakeable alibi. I could tell them. The man is a snake, that's how. When the occasion demands, he can float that sixteen stone like a ballet dancer, and those leg of beef arms can sweep like a rapier. As to his turgid brain, he's managed to fool the examiners into awarding him two college degrees. Not one. Two. That's how dumb he is.

Well, he doesn't fool me. I've seen that sleepy act before. He blinked owlishly at my greeting.

'What is this about the record?' he queried. 'Aren't all of these witnesses here enough for you?'

He waved an arm around the empty room. I wasn't comfortable.

'Just so's they're paying attention,' I grumbled.

'Oh they are, they are,' he assured, hunching even further down in his chair. 'Detective Second Grade Schultz tells me he ran across you today.'

'It'll all be in that file in front of you,' I evaded.

Again the heavy nod.

'H'm. All, you say? I prefer to say some of it. Some of it is in this file right here, as you correctly surmise. Tell you what's bothering me, Preston. It's the stuff that isn't on the file. Why don't we talk about that?'

I shrugged, pulling out cigarets.

'I don't know what else you want. I told Schultzie all I know. Which,' I emphasised heavily, 'is nothing.'

'Schultz is a good officer,' he intoned. 'Good man, too. Likes to protect the individual. Look at the way he turned you loose, today. That was nice of him, wouldn't you say?'

'I don't see what else he could do,' I declared, all innocence. 'I was just a man who happened along. What they call a bystander, isn't that the term?'

'Is it? I wouldn't know. If it'd been me, I'd have tossed you in the can, just on principle. I don't care for this bystander definition, not when the bystander is you. You are not one of life's bystanders, Preston. You are more the pitcher-in type. More of a make-things-happen kind of man. Were you making things happen there today?'

The lids above his eyes had now made contact with the pouches below, and he was plainly unconscious, for all the world to see.

All the world except me.

'If you mean did I knock off the late Mr. Hall, the answer is no.'

'Tut tut,' he hemmed. 'Who said anything about knocking anybody off? Your words, not mine. No, it just seemed to me kind of strange, how a character like you chanced to be along at what they call the critical moment. You take my point?'

I could hear his words, but that wasn't his point at all. There was something else here. Something I knew nothing about. Something that had prompted a busy detective sergeant to take over a case that I had no doubt was being ably handled by one of his squad. The only way to get answers is to ask questions.

'Mind telling me something?' I queried. 'Why are you taking a hand in this game? Last I heard, Schultzie was pretty well thought of around here.'

The eyes opened one millimetre.

'Glad you asked me that. I was going to come round to it, anyway. Fact is, Preston, I am going to tie you into this somehow. And then, I am going to nail you to the wall.'

I didn't understand that at all. I didn't like the sound of it, either.

'Mind telling me why?'

'My pleasure,' he assured me. 'You see, it shapes up like this. Here we have this guy bumped off. He doesn't seem to be anybody much. Name of Ben Hall. Here we have Detective Schultz looking into things, doing a good job, too. Schultz always does a good job. Then suddenly, guess what happens?'

He looked to me for reaction. All he got was puzzlement.

'Why ask me?'

'I ask you because I think you know, is why I ask you,' and his voice suddenly developed a nasty edge. 'What happens is, Detective Schultz gets a telephone call. From the mayor's office, no less. Not from here, not from the chief of police, nor the commissioner, from Hizzonner's office. I don't have to tell you what the message said, now do I?'

'Yes, you do,' I contradicted. 'I don't know what you're talking about.'

'I don't believe you, but let it pass. I'll tell you anyway. The message was short. It said, lay off Preston. That's what it said. Now, how do you like them apples?'

If I'd felt uneasy before, I was downright unhappy now.

'Not much,' I admitted. 'What do you suppose it means?'

He shrugged his massive shoulders.

'Suppose? I don't have to suppose. I know what it means. And you know what it means. It means you have some kind of political pull in this village, and the politicians don't want you disturbed. That's what it means. The point is, why? Why should we lay off you? As far as we know, you're clean. But this changes everything. It means we were wrong. It means you're up to your dirty neck in something, and we are supposed to leave you to get on with it. Well now, here's the message, and you can take it back to your courthouse friends. We don't play favors here. Not only that, we don't take orders from them or anybody else. It gets worse. So far as I am concerned, you are not even going to get a square shake. Any dirty tricks I can pull, any little unorthodox methods that come to hand, I am going to throw them right at you. Tell that to your fixer friends.'

He glowered at me with dislike, and that was a new feeling between us. I'd had trouble with Randall, on and off, over the years, but we'd never had this particular fence to jump.

'Gil — ' I began.

' — Sergeant will do — ' he cut in.

'Listen, I don't know any more about this than you do. I don't have any in with the politicians, and you know it. We go back a long way. I wouldn't say we were bosom pals. I wouldn't say there haven't been times when we didn't get along, but this is different. This is not my style, not the way I operate. And you know me better.'

He listened, with no change of expression.

'Back a long way? Not your style? I know you better?' He repeated my own phrases as questions, rattling them out at machine-gun pace. 'Let me tell you something. In this job, a man never knows anybody. He might think he does, and then it happens. Oh my, my. Look what so-and-so did, what a surprise. Who would have thought it. Like old Mr. Hoffer. Runs a candy store on the corner of the block where I grew up. I knew him since I was five years old, and he was a sweet old man. Last week he set fire to the store. His wife was inside it at the time, and now that sweet old man has been arraigned on fourteen counts. Don't talk to me about knowing people. The longer I'm around, the less I know. I don't pretend to understand why people do things. It's enough for me that they do them. Why, is for courtrooms. My business is with facts. And the fact is, somebody is trying to interfere with this squad, and you're mixed up in it. Be told, Preston. I will stretch you out on a fence when the sun is high, and I want you to repeat that to your friends.'

I made one last try.

'I understand how you feel,' I assured him, keeping my tone unemotional. 'But I repeat that I don't know anything. Everything is exactly the way I told it to Schultz. That's all there is to it.'

'And I say you're a liar,' he replied, almost conversationally. 'I say you're in it up to your neck. And explain this one. If you're just a bystander, what were you doing poking around in Hall's apartment this afternoon? What were you doing beating up on the manager, and scaring the hell out of him?'

I reached across the desk for an ashtray. It gave me a few seconds in which to absorb this information, and try to assimilate it into the rest of the material. In my own mind I was fairly certain of what had happened. Harrison Page, the distinguished wine merchant, had hired me to do a job. Either he, or one of his minions, had thought it no more than a routine matter to pressurise the political machine into ensuring that I had a clear field. Probably thought he was doing me a favor, a gesture of business goodwill. But my town doesn't run like that, certainly not where the Homicide Bureau is involved. All that such a move would produce would be trouble. Trouble in the shape of Detective Sergeant Gil Randall, who was now staring at my ashtray routine and waiting for a reply. It hadn't taken him long to catch up with the goings-on at the Almira Apartments. Did he know about Still-Life Portraits Inc. as well? Worse, did he know about my involvement there? Because if he did, I was already facing a handsome list of charges, ranging from concealment of a felony right up to accessory after the fact of murder.

'I am not involved in this,' I insisted doggedly, 'but people seem set on getting me involved. Did you see the paper, did you see the tee vee news? First they mention Hall, then me. Every time. Nobody says I'm involved. Nobody accuses me of anything. They just stick these pictures on, one after the other, and leave people to draw their own conclusions.'

'Oh dearie me,' he said sourly. 'Aren't people nasty? I just bet you cried all the way home. What's so unusual? You've been picked on before.'

'Yes, and it doesn't bother me,' I agreed. 'But this is different. This is family business. Those guys don't pick on people, they kill them.'

He came back fast.

'Who says they're in it? Nothing about that in the paper.'

'I was tipped off,' I shrugged.

'Who and when?' he shot out.

'Tip Hatch of the Sentinel. I went round to Sam's for a beer, just after it happened. He bumped into me, and told me to watch my step. I checked around, and it turns out Hall is a Halsetti, from San Francisco way. That got me interested, and fast. If those people get the idea I'm in this, they won't sit around asking questions. They'll shoot first. I thought I'd ask around, see if I could come up with anything. It's called self-protection. And if you don't like it, that's too bad. It's my neck that's on the line.'

I put a little suggestion into my tone, for extra conviction. If it made any impression on my audience there was nothing in his face to tell me.

'Why push the manager around?'

'I didn't,' I denied outright. 'And if he says I did, he's a liar. Guy was drunk as a skunk when I left him. The only time I touched him was when I had to stick a hand out to prevent him falling on his face.'

'H'm.' He reflected on this. Then, 'You poked around the apartment.'

'I certainly did. But I didn't find anything. You people had already cleaned it out.'

'And what have you done since? Who else did you beat up on?'

I made a face.

'There's nowhere else for me to go. Once I realised I was on a cold trail with Hall, I got back to my own work. I'm looking for a man named Horace Winters. He's a bond-jumper — '

A huge hand waved me to silence.

'I know what he is. Let's just stick to one investigation at a time. So, the way you tell it, you are like the driven snow on this?'

'Exactly like it,' I agreed.

'Then you don't know where she is?'

'She?'

Randall sighed with heavy patience.

'The little girl. Angela Halsetti. You didn't find her?'

At least I didn't have to play at being innocent over that.

'No idea,' I replied definitely. 'I didn't even know there was a little girl in this, until the manager told me about her. She's probably holed up somewhere, scared half to death.'

'Thanks,' he returned. 'I hadn't thought

of that. But you wouldn't know anything about her?'

I thought about those photographs, and the terrified child looking into the camera. But I couldn't know about that. Not unless I knew about the Luckman murder. Randall would know all about it soon enough. Besides, all I had was a theory. I couldn't swear the violated child had been Angela Halsetti.

'Nothing,' I confirmed. 'And, by the way, I have a theory.'

'A theory?' and he made no attempt to conceal his disgust. 'A theory. Look, this here is a police department, not some college seminar on Crime in Society. We don't use theories, we use facts. Dates, places, guns, blood samples, stuff like that. Theory? All right, let's hear it.'

My prime concern was to restore my relationship with the department, and my mind had been searching around for ways of doing it.

'Suppose this Halsetti killing is mob business,' I suggested, leaning forward for emphasis. 'They're not dumb, those people, not these days. They know what a small department you have here, how pressed you are for manpower' — good ploy this, and a favorite topic with any ranking police officer — 'suppose they planted the idea with you that I knew more than I was telling? Not in an obvious way. Not with an anonymous telephone call, but by the surefire method of warning you off? They would know how much ice that would cut in this particular department. They would know what your reaction would be. It could help them. You might even put a tail on me. And all the manpower you waste, all the time you spend thinking about me, chasing around after me, that is so much less time, so much less manpower for you to use getting after the truth. It may sound pretty fanciful, but it's a thought.'

He didn't reply at once, and I had a half-hope that he might like it. I liked it, but then, it was my brain-child.

'It's not impossible,' he grunted finally. 'It has the kind of twisted thinking behind it that these people seem to go in for. Not that I'm buying it, don't get that impression. All I'm saying is, it's not impossible. That does not mean you are off the hook. What I said at the beginning still goes. Nobody warns us off, and you are still all we have. You're walking on eggs, Preston. Don't break any. Don't even crack one tiny piece of shell, or I'll have you breaking rocks, and believe me, they're harder. Now get out of here.'

With the mood he was in, I didn't wait to be told a second time. At the door I said

'Oh, by the way — '

' — well? — '

' — if anybody should run across this Horace Winters — '

'OUT,' he roared.

I went.

7

After a fitful night I rolled into the office shortly before ten a.m. Florence Digby raised her eyebrows.

'Couldn't you sleep?'

'And good morning to you also,' I told her grumpily. 'Don't you have anything better to do than watch television on my time?'

The word-processor was her new soft spot, and I could always get to her by accusing her of playing with it like a space-invaders toy.

'Somebody has to do some of the work around here,' she retorted. 'If it was left to the president of the corporation, everything would be covered in rust in a week.'

A sound from the inner office caused my head to swivel round.

'We're being burgled,' I informed her. 'They must have walked right past you to get in there.'

'Wrong,' she corrected. 'Those are the

sounds of Mr. Sam Thompson. He's either reading the newspapers or your mail.'

'Then I'd better go stop him.' I didn't bother to remonstrate with her about letting him through. Somewhere inside the Digby armoury there is a chink, and Thompson seems to have the secret of it. I used to bother about it, try to figure it out, but that was back in the days when I still thought it was possible to understand women. 'Anything on my man Winters?'

'No,' she denied. 'But Mr. Andrews called again. That is Mr. Andrews of — '

' — of Andrews, Clark and Andrews, yes I know. Man seems to spend half his life telephoning me.'

'And in office hours too,' she added sweetly. 'Working time. Isn't that old-fashioned of him? He didn't know whether to believe me when I told him you hadn't arrived yet. Shall I call him back?'

'Not yet, let me deal with Thompson first.'

I went through into my immaculate office. Correction. I went through into what is normally my immaculate office. Today it looked like the inside of a corporation garbage truck after a dust storm. The far from immaculate Thompson was sitting behind my desk, in my chair, with sheets of newsprint spread in all directions, including the floor. There was cigaret ash everywhere except in the ashtray. He looked up and nodded, making no attempt to shift.

'What are you doing about all this crime, Preston?' he queried. 'It says here street muggings are up nineteen per cent on last year. Rape went up twenty-four per cent, armed robbery by eleven. Seems to me you ought to be out there waging some kind of crusade. Assisted by me, at very reasonable rates.'

'You want a job, Sam?'

'Command me,' he invited.

'Then you can start by cleaning up this office. Get it looking the way it was before you got here.'

'That's janitors' work,' he objected.

'Then be a janitor,' I said nastily. 'Or do I call a cop and have him book you on a vagrancy charge?'

He heaved and shuffled his bulky frame up from the chair, and began to reassemble the papers. I sat in the visitor's chair, thinking.

There are two major areas of criminal activity, and they rarely overlap. On the one hand there is the one-timer. This covers the big financial swindles, the frauds, the crimes of passion and so forth. Mostly, indeed almost exclusively, crimes in this category are committed by otherwise ordinary people. Strictly non-professional. On the other hand is the whole crime-range, staffed by people for whom crime is a way of life. It isn't such a bad life, for people who won't work. They coast along, picking up a little here, a little there, sometimes a big one. Every now and then they get tagged, but that's all part of it, and the odds are heavily in their favor. They are a fraternity, everybody knows everybody else, or at least knows of them. They know who's doing what, and to whom. They even have their own rules, and they won't tolerate people who step out of line. Shooting, knifing and general mayhem are all acceptable activities. Larceny, in all its guises, is their everyday currency, along with breaking and entering, extortion, and second-storey work. But there are lines drawn, and I'm not talking about what the romantics call 'honor among thieves'. This is strictly for the sob-columns. A thief is a thief, and he'll steal from anybody, including his own kind. No, what I'm talking about is offenses against children. That is the one area where the hard men are just as unctuous as any church leader. A character who will knife a storekeeper without compunction, or turn a machine-gun on a security van, goes pale at the thought of people who molest children. Woe betide the convicted offender who winds up in jail. His chances of coming out the way he was when he went in are almost nil. In fact, his chance of coming out at all is no better than fifty fifty.

Sitting there, I was cogitating as to how I could turn that to my advantage. George Luckman, deceased, had been in the blue movie business. The fact was probably well known, and no one would care too much. It was my guess he was also a blackmailer, and that would raise no eyebrows either. But I wondered to what extent it was known on the street that a child had been involved. That would put a different complexion on everything. That would make whoever killed Luckman a public hero. It was no part of my thinking that anyone would turn him in. Quite the reverse. Everyone would see it as their solemn obligation to ensure that the murderer escaped. But they wouldn't be able to resist talking about it. Not to the law, not to the newspapers, but to each other. Gossip is an essential part of the life of that community, and like any bunch of legitimate workers, they gossip about their own trade.

It was possible that they didn't yet know about Luckman's murder, but that could only be a matter of hours. It seemed to me that if I could be sure the news about what kind of pictures he was making hit the street while news of his sudden demise was still warm, I might be able to pick up some useful information.

Not me, personally. For one thing, I was wearing a tie, and a tie will hush all conversation in certain quarters. Sam Thompson, now, was a different proposition altogether. He was a familiar figure around the bars and cafes of the lower strata. It wasn't that I expected anyone to confide in Sam. It was rather that people just wouldn't bother to guard their tongue while he was within earshot.

'How'd you like to visit a few bars at my expense?'

It was certainly one of the most unnecessary questions I ever asked.

Thompson ceased his smoothing at that morning's Globe, and beamed across at me.

'That is very sweet music you are playing today,' he said suspiciously, 'but I get this feeling I may have to kill somebody. Why all the largesse?'

'There is a catch,' I admitted. 'You have to stay upright, and you have to keep listening. Hard.'

He nodded, understanding.

'Did I ever show you my ears? Finest in town. Listen, I have commendations about these ears — '

'Just keep 'em open,' I instructed. 'Now, this is the story.'

I told him what was going on. Well, most of it. I left out the Harrison Page involvement. It isn't that I don't trust Sam. It's just that my business with Page was one-to-one and I had enough sense to keep it that way. But I did tell him about the visitors from San Francisco. He didn't like it too well.

'H'm,' he muttered. 'Guns. And from out of town. You wouldn't be perhaps exposing me to any danger, would you Preston?'

'Perhaps,' I shrugged. 'But it shouldn't amount to anything you can't handle. Those people are not after you.'

'Maybe not, but I know the type. If they start to get excited, they might just forget that.'

'Then don't get them excited,' I advised. 'Anyway, there's no reason why you should run across them at all. I only mentioned them so you'll know they're around.'

'It's going to inhibit my drinking,' he

mused. 'Can't afford to get drowsy, if those characters are in the background.'

Which was another reason I'd saved them till last.

'The thing to remember is that they are just making noise. They don't really know anything. Not yet, anyway. No, your prime concern is this Luckman thing. I have to tie it in with the Hall killing. Maybe the same man killed them both. I just don't know, Sam. I'm groping around in the dark. Just let me have anything you hear.'

'I'll need some cash.'

Peeling off bills, I handed them over and his eyes gleamed.

'How'll I find you?' he queried. 'You can be a very elusive character.'

'Just call Florence. Tell her to put it on her space-machine.'

'Huh?'

He didn't get the allusion.

'Private joke. Don't worry about it. Well, don't let me keep you. The bars are open.'

'Space machine?' he muttered to himself, shuffling out.

From outside came the mutter of voices, then the outer door closed, and Florence buzzed me.

'Mr. Preston, I know you must be very busy,' inflection there that I didn't care for, 'but may I remind you about Mr. Andrews? If he has an assignment for us, he won't keep it for ever. There are other firms in this city who would be only too eager to return his call.'

I was about to chew off a small piece of her head, when I pulled on the reins. Florence was not out of line. If anyone was to be accused of that, it has to be me. She didn't know I was working for Harrison Page, and I had no intention of telling her. Florence runs a legitimate office. For her, an assignment means a case file, cash receipts, expenses, the internal revenue. That was not the way Mr. Page worked. He ran an all-cash, no records kind of business, and he wouldn't expect me to break the pattern. So, just for once, I was going to have to deceive Miss Digby. I would have to let her think that my interest in Benny Hall's murder was purely speculative, and in the hope that there might be a grateful client at the end. In those circumstances, I had no excuse for not following up a possible job offer with Mr. Andrews.

'You're right, Florence,' I conceded. 'Get him for me, please.'

A minute later, he was on the line.

'Mr. Preston?'

'Good morning Mr. Andrews,' I greeted. 'I'm sorry you've had a little difficulty in contacting me. I was too late up to make that ten o'clock meeting you suggested. Things have been kind of hectic around here.'

'Just so, just so,' he replied. 'However, I hope you will find it possible to call and see me at this office. Shall we say in one hour? Eleven thirty?'

I hesitated, but not for long. So far as the outside world knew, I was a man without employment, unless you counted the elusive Horace. It would look odd if I turned away an offer of genuine work.

'I'll be there,' I promised, and hung up.

Florence Digby thawed out to the extent of one half-smile of approval when

I announced that I was leaving to see Mr. Andrews.

'If you could possibly avoid tripping over any bodies on your way,' she suggested sweetly.

'I'll keep away from elevators,' I told her, and went out.

Andrews, Clark and Andrews are one of those old institutions that seem to have been around since the gold rush. Not big, not fancy, but old and well-established. Other firms make more splash, get their names in the paper all the time, clamor for attention. They have go-getting titles like Flash, Getrich and Snide, and they occupy ten-roomed suites of offices full of eager young pushers. They represent the dream. Andrews, Clark and Andrews represent the reality. When some elderly millionaire passes away, it is their name that appears in the papers. Not on Page One. Not in the big courtroom cases, but tucked away at the bottom of Page Eight, under 'Enquiries should be forwarded to'. That's the kind of people they are. I was more than curious to know what they could possibly want with someone like me. They had four rooms in the heart of the business section, and there was none of that get-up-and-go about the premises. Or the staff.

An elderly woman with gray hair tucked away in a bun looked at me with motherly interest. She should have been home in her slippers, watching Today's Recipe.

'Ah yes, Mr. Preston. Mr. Andrews is expecting you. Won't you go through, please?'

She pointed, and I went through thank you. Andrews was a very old fifty, with pince-nez on a raddled nose, and a rusty black suit that didn't quite squeak when he stood to receive me.

'Mr. Preston. Good of you to come. Please have a seat.'

There was nothing rusty about his eyes, which were small and brilliant. I parked in the chair opposite, a massive leather wing-back, which invited instant sleep. As I began to sink into it, I shifted my weight forward, to maintain some kind of alertness.

'You are quite right of course,' he

remarked, watching me. 'That chair is far too comfortable. I keep meaning to replace it with something more postural. Are you all right, perched like that?'

'Fine thank you,' I assured him. 'What can I do for you Mr. Andrews?'

'Ah yes,' he nodded. 'As to that.'

Then he leaned back, pressed his fingertips together, and went silent. Behind him, an old-fashioned clock ticked loudly away. In that hushed room, it sounded like a road-hammer. His next words seemed almost shouted.

'It is my understanding Mr. Preston that you are a man who is to be trusted to respect confidentiality. Would that be correct?'

This was a man to whom words meant something. I chose mine with care when I replied.

'To a large extent,' I agreed. 'But I have limits. I won't, for example, keep quiet if I have knowledge of a crime. What I mean is, if the person who hires me proves to be a murderer, I will turn them in. I don't believe in that much confidentiality.'

He nodded, as though expecting

something of the kind.

'Quite. Oh, quite. But this would not necessarily mean that you would report to the police on every law-infringement you encountered. I mean, for example, if an innocent person would be likely to suffer.'

This line of questioning was not casual. Mr. Andrews was not a casual type of man.

'I wouldn't want to commit myself on a hypothesis,' I hedged. 'I would have to be presented with a real situation before I could decide.'

'That is quite satisfactory,' and we had some more nodding. 'In fact, I should have found it mildly disturbing if you had said anything different. Very well, let us talk about a real situation. One that involves a child. If I judge you correctly, Mr. Preston, it would be your attitude that the best interests of a child would normally outweigh other considerations?'

But my mind was already beginning to race, juggling possibilities.

'Normally,' I replied with care. 'Yes normally. But even then, I would prefer to hear the facts.'

He spotted a fragment of cotton on his coatsleeve, and picked it off with meticulous care, rolling it into a ball and dropping it out of sight.

'Facts, then.' Pursing his lips, he began to intone. 'You were present yesterday, quite by chance, when a man was found dead. Murdered. His name was reported in the press as Hall. The name is not correct. His name was Halsetti. He was a man of most unsavory reputation and background. In fact, my advisers tell me his whole family are petty criminals, and are well known to the San Francisco Police Department. I see you are somewhat surprised.'

It hadn't seemed necessary to wear my poker face in this company, and my expression had obviously given something away. Mr. Andrews was assuming that I was surprised at his news. He was wrong there, because none of this was news to me at all. My surprise was to hear it coming from him, but I didn't bother to enlighten him. He was clearly enjoying himself.

'A little,' I confessed. 'Please go on.'

'Halsetti had with him a thirteen year old girl. He told everyone she was his daughter, and the police are anxious to find her. They are naturally, and quite properly, concerned for her welfare, but they are working on false information. The girl is not his daughter at all, and her name is neither Hall nor Halsetti. It is Stefano, Angela Stefano, and her real parents are respected people. They live in San Francisco, and are, I believe, quite comfortably off.'

This was news indeed. If I hadn't been sitting on the edge of the chair when he began, I'd have been doing it now.

'Are you saying this Halsetti kidnapped the girl? And our police don't know about it? I don't believe I could keep quiet about that, Mr. Andrews. Kidnapping is a federal offense, and it would be more than my licence is worth for me to conceal it. Particularly when the subject is under-age. I think we had better stop the conversation right now. You haven't really told me anything so far, and so I'm not concealing anything. If you go on with this, I shall have to report it.'

I seemed to be hitting the right note, to judge from the satisfied look on my listener's face.

'Excellent,' he purred. 'I was told that you are a man of nice judgement, Mr. Preston. Your present reaction would seem to bear that out. However, you misread me. In some ways I almost wish you did not. Kidnapping, however reprehensible, would in some ways be preferable to this current situation. There is no question of it. The girl, Angela Stefano, ran away with Halsetti entirely of her own volition. Not a new situation, as I am sure you must know from your own experience. A young, impressionable girl, flattered by the attentions of a man old enough to be her father. No doubt this Halsetti had a certain flashy charm. Plenty of money to spend, a fast car, all those things which are calculated to turn a youngster's head.'

'Why didn't the parents put a stop to it?' I queried.

'How?' he returned sharply. 'A girl of that age is too old to be locked up. It isn't possible to accompany her everywhere

161

she goes. She has to go out to school, to youth activities, church and so forth. If she is prepared to lie to her parents consistently, they have no way of checking on every movement. I am sure the Stefanos did whatever they could, but in a case like this, it wouldn't be enough. Certainly it wasn't effective with Angela.'

I'd been searching around in my head for a phrase, and I thought I'd found it.

'Still an offense though, surely? I forget the exact words, but it's something like 'making away with a minor, against the wishes of the parents.' Isn't that it?'

'The words are wrong but the essence is correct,' he agreed. 'But the Stefanos do not wish to attract that kind of publicity to their daughter. I asked the same question myself. The answer was, and as a parent myself I could understand it, that the damage to the girl's community reputation would be beyond repair. The police might find Halsetti, charge him, have him committed to prison. Where would that leave Angela? She is an intelligent, popular girl, they tell me. Reasonable school grades, irreproachable family background. As a kidnap victim, she would have attracted only sympathy and understanding. But, as a young woman who voluntarily ran away with a known criminal, everything would be washed away, and permanently. Sinners may be forgiven for a ritualistic hour each Sunday, Mr. Preston. On the other six days they are consigned to the outer reaches of hell. The more respectable the community, the more vicious the treatment. I think you would have to agree with that?'

He looked at me with a question in his eyes.

I nodded.

'Unfortunately, yes. And I think I can see where we're going. You want me to find Angela, and return her to the family. Is that it?'

'Not entirely,' he qualified. 'Find her, yes. Talk to her, if possible. See if you can persuade her to go home. But no force. Once we know where she is, the family will come at once and try to persuade her. The fear is, you see, that she may

163

rebel permanently. I don't know the figures, and you are probably better informed than I, but the number of young girls who disappear each year must be astronomical.'

He stopped talking, and there was that silence again, with that old clock ticking away. Mr. Andrews was assuming my thoughtfulness to indicate that I was absorbing what he had told me. He was only partly right. My mind was also filled with other facts, other images. I was seeing again the terrified kid in the photographs. There wasn't one fact in my possession to confirm that it was Angela Stefano being abused. It could all be just coincidence, and there were two girls of the same age mixed up in the same case at the same time. But I wasn't buying it. I like to play the odds, and the odds in favour of two girls were all against.

I didn't want this job, and for many reasons. The chief one was that I didn't see how I could keep the Stefanos from finding out the truth, even if I succeeded in finding Angela. All I would be delivering was bad news, any way you looked at it. On the other hand, I knew I couldn't refuse. Mr. Andrews would only go and hire someone else, and then I'd have to contend with opposition. Another pair of feet would be trampling all over the territory, disturbing things, upsetting people. I couldn't permit that.

No, I was going to have to fall in line, like it or not. Depending on the way things turned out, I could always make a grand gesture at the end. Like refusing to take the Stefanos' money, for instance. That would help to salve my conscience a little, and it certainly would put me in very large with Andrews, Clark and Andrews.

'Are you having difficulty in making up your mind, Mr. Preston?'

The question was put quietly.

'Oh no, no,' I denied. 'It's just that I don't quite know how to put it to you. This is a big city, Mr. Andrews, and there are bigger ones only a few miles away. My chance of finding one thirteen year old girl are small. Very small. I don't like to build up people's hopes.'

'That is very commendable,' he assented,

'and realistic too. The point is, are you willing to try?'

I almost had to force the next words out.

'Yes. I'll start asking around. What about the police?'

He didn't like that.

'Police? What about them?'

'They always like to know what I'm up to,' I explained. 'What's my story, if they question my sudden interest in Angela Stefano? Don't forget, they still think she's Halsetti's daughter.'

'H'm. Yes.' He pondered for a moment, then gave it up. 'Well, you have been dealing with the police for years, Mr. Preston. I am sure your native resourcefulness will provide a satisfactory explanation. I thought you might find this of assistance.'

'This' was a check for five hundred dollars, already made out in my name. Mr. Andrews was accustomed to having his own way.

Five minutes later I was out in the heat.

Me and my native resourcefulness.

8

There was a young man leaning against the car, reading a newspaper. He wore a sober gray business suit, white silk shirt and a striped tie. The soft blonde hair was clipped neatly, all around a cheery, unblemished face. He smiled widely at my approach, letting the sun flash from gleaming, regular teeth. This was the man in the ads, the one who bought the shirts, used the mouthwash, drove the big car, but only in long-shot. The rest of him was spoiled by the eyes. The smile didn't reach up there, nor did the sun. The eyes were the cold slate of winter, bleak and flat. He smelled of death. Close to him, I almost shivered.

'It is Mr. Preston, isn't it? Mr. Mark Preston?'

'It is. Who are you?'

He shrugged non-commitally.

'Nobody. I carry pieces of paper around for a friend. Got one for you. It has a number on it. My friend would like you to call him. Use a pay-phone.'

He thrust a note into my hand, and folded his paper.

'And that's it?' I queried.

'That's it,' he confirmed. 'Have a nice day.'

He flipped me a small salute with the paper and strolled away. I watched him until he reached a parked car further down the street. He sat in it, and the car moved away. I'd seen it before, in the garage beneath Harrison Page's house.

I located a pay-phone, and waited outside while a perspiring fat woman conducted a non-stop harangue against some unfortunate. When she was through, she didn't even say goodbye. She simply slammed the phone down and stalked out, glaring at me.

I pushed buttons, and the receiver at the other end was lifted at once. Harrison Page's voice said

'Don't use any names. I know who you are. Do you know who you're talking to?'

'Yes,' I replied, 'I spotted the car. The one your messenger boy used.' There was no necessity for me to mention that, but I did it deliberately. It might make Page think the boy had been careless. If I could spot the car, so might others. Maybe I would get the boy in trouble. I certainly hoped so.

'All right. Tell me what's been going on. I hear you've been busy.'

I'd always known I would have to talk to Page eventually, but I hadn't bargained on it quite so soon, nor at such short notice. What I'd been hoping for was time to think. Time in which to arrange my mind, decide what it was safe to leave out. Page had hired me to do a job, but I was under no illusion that he would leave it at that. He would have his own people out, listening, asking questions. They would also be doing other things, if he thought it was necessary, things it might be better for me not to know about.

Like George Luckman, no longer available to cover all social functions.

It had been a natural assumption that the killings of Hall and Luckman were related. Indeed, it was as near certain as can be. But that didn't have to mean there was only one killer involved. Page was after the man who murdered Hall. The killing of Luckman, a few hours later, might have been the work of the same man, but then again it might just have been done at Page's behest. A little tidying-up work, a good-will gesture to the boys up north. I had no way of knowing, but here I was, talking to the man himself, and being expected to report. How could I judge his reaction if he learned that I was the first on the scene after Luckman departed this life? Might that make me some kind of risk in Page's super-careful mind?

'I'm not hearing anything,' he rasped. 'What's going on?'

'Sorry,' I blurted. 'There was someone standing too close. I had to get rid of them, in case they listened.'

It was the kind of thinking that would appeal to him.

'Kay. Let's have it.'

I swallowed, and knew I could not keep Luckman out of it. He was the key. Without him, there was no blackmail, no blue movie setup, no explanation of Angela's role.

But first, there were the Halsettis.

'There are two soldiers down here from Hall's branch of the family,' I began, 'but maybe you knew that?'

'Maybe. What about them?'

'They waved guns at me, sounded off a bit. They're looking for blood, and I don't want it to be mine.'

'H'm.' He thought for a moment, then 'Kay, I'll speak to some people. Tell 'em to lay off you. What else you got?'

I took a deep breath, like jumping into dark, cold water.

'Hall was mixed up with a man named Luckman, George Luckman. A photographer. He also ran a blackmail racket, and made dirty movies.'

'Made?' he interrupted sharply. 'You mean he quit?'

'I mean he's dead,' I said outright. 'Somebody filled him full of holes yesterday afternoon, late. I found him.'

'Same gun? Same as killed Benny?'

'I don't know. The police will find that out fast enough, once they find Luckman.

They may be on to it now, I wouldn't know.'

Silence again.

'So you didn't report it.'

'Certainly not. I had no business to be there. As long as I'm working for you, the last people I want to talk to are the police. Besides, there's another angle. Hall's daughter.'

'The kid? What about her? And where is she?'

'I wish I knew. Everybody in town seems to be looking for her. She's either keeping well out of sight, or somebody else is keeping her that way. This blackmail I mentioned, the girl Angela was involved.'

'Involved? How? Spell it out.'

Page wasn't going to like this part. His sense of shock at the mere suggestion of child-abuse would be as genuine and heartfelt as that of the main street storekeeper.

'They were using her. With men. I've seen the photographs.'

I kept it short and simple. My listener wouldn't need any more. He said something I didn't understand, something low and emotional. Perhaps it was Greek.

'You couldna made no mistake about this?'

'Not unless there are two young girls the same age, mixed up with the same two men. I've never seen Angela, it's true, but I'd lay heavy odds it has to be her in the pictures.'

There was more animation in his voice when he spoke next.

'But his own daughter, for crissakes. It don't make no sense. What kind of a man would do that to his own kid? Any kid is bad enough, bottom of the barrel, but a man's own flesh and blood. No. You have to be wrong about this. It's some other poor little mite.'

A bluebottle fly droned lazily in, and sat on the dialling instructions, looking at me. Putrefaction was everywhere today.

'That's something else I found out. Angela is not Hall's daughter. She comes from a respectable family, and he talked her into running away with him. That should make it easier to accept.'

I wished I could see Page's face. It's very difficult, having to impart vital information of this kind over the telephone, without having any way to judge its impact.

He didn't say he didn't believe me, not in so many words. But when he came back his voice was incredulous.

'Not his daughter? Where'd you get that?'

'From what they call an unimpeachable source,' I replied, and went on to tell him about Mr. Gettysburg Andrews.

'I'll check it out, but it sounds for real,' he admitted grudgingly. 'So how does it shape? If this Luckman was on the black, and little Benny was mixed up in it, could be the same guy took care of both of 'em. Yes?'

'It begins to look that way,' I agreed. 'When you and I talked yesterday, you said yourself this was amateur night. Believe me, any one of those men in the pictures I saw would pay through the nose to keep them quiet. It may have got too heavy for one of them and he took his own way out.'

'Yeah,' he assented heavily. 'O.K. Better let me take a look at those pictures.'

'I haven't got them,' I said reluctantly, knowing he would not like it.

'Mind telling me why?' he asked suspiciously. 'You wouldn't be holding out on me, would you? That wouldn't be too smart.'

'No, I wouldn't,' I assured him. 'I looked at it like this.'

I went into my spiel about how the men in the photographs were almost certainly ordinary citizens, and that the chances of my ever tracing them were practically nil. The police would find it hard enough, with all their resources. He listened, and again I wished I could have seen his face.

'All right,' he breathed grudgingly. 'I don't like it, but all right. I can see you got a point. Maybe the cops will come good.'

'There's something else,' I added, and this I hoped he would like a lot better. 'If one of those men is the killer, then the police will get him, sooner or later. But I want the police to take them all. The murder of Benny Hall isn't the only crime on offer here. Each and every one of those guys is raping a child. In my book, they should all be locked up.'

It was the kind of thinking that would appeal to him, and it had one further merit. I meant it.

'This could change things, you understand,' he said.

'Change them what way?'

'Money-way,' he retorted. 'If the cops pick up this clown, you talked yourself out of five thousand dollars. The grand you got, you keep, but if you don't finish the rest of this movie, that's it. Y'unnerstand?'

'Got it,' I replied, 'and that's fair enough. There's one other thing I'd like to mention. Speaking of cops, I'm in trouble down there.'

'So? Whaddya want, my condolences?'

I was busy figuring out a form of words which might persuade him into action.

'You told me, and you made it very plain, that no one was to be able to put a connection between us. I've kept my end.'

'You're suggesting something. What is it?'

'Somebody your end seems to think it's necessary for me to have no interference from the police. They put in a word, through the mayor's office. The police don't like it, and they don't like me. Your name hasn't been mentioned, or even thought about, so far as I know. But the fact remains. The boys at headquarters think some kind of a fix is in, and I'm mixed up in it. If they get mad enough, they might start to dig. If they do, they might turn up something. I thought you'd better know now, because it won't be my doing.'

If he was upset, his voice gave nothing away.

'Kay, you made your point. I'll toss some sand around.'

There was a click, and I was looking into a dead phone.

'Just like that,' I muttered sourly.

The bluebottle shrugged. I took a swipe at him, but he rose two lazy inches into the air, and settled back as soon as the danger was past.

'The hell with you,' I told him.

'You talking to me, mac?'

A burly man with a two-day shadow thrust his face close to mine as I stepped out of the booth.

'No,' I assured him. 'I was talking to — er — ' I looked back into the booth, where my late adversary sat watching smugly. ' — er — just talking to myself.'

'Crazy people. The world is lousy with crazy people,' grumbled shave-face, counting out change.

The sun was really settling into its task now, its task being to turn anything made of stone or metal into furnace material. Anything made of flesh and blood, such as people, turned either into walking automatons or the nearest bar. I decided I could just about make it to Sam's, along with, as I soon discovered, half the male population.

'No grub left,' confided Sam. 'Been like Christmas in here.'

'It's the snow,' I explained, carrying my beer off into a corner.

If I'd been hoping for a little privacy, I'd come to the wrong place. On a day like that, any place would have been the wrong place. A man elbowed his way to

178

where I was leaning against the wall. It seemed to be my week for bumping into Tip Hatch.

'Hi,' I greeted. 'Anything new on my murder?'

He looked slightly puzzled for a moment, then his face cleared.

'Oh, that murder,' he exclaimed. 'No, nothing much. Not that I've heard anyway. Must be nice to be a one-murder-at-a-time character like you. We of the media are in the wholesale business. Three other citizens cashed in since last we met.'

This might be my chance to learn something.

'Really? You must've been busy.'

He wagged his head tiredly.

'A little. The two last night were nothing. Just a couple kids trying to hold up a supermarket. When the law turned up, they decided to go out in a blaze of glory.'

'And did they?'

He made a gesture of distaste.

'Oh, they went out all right. I didn't notice much glory.'

'You mentioned another one,' I prompted.

The doleful expression went away.

'Better. Much better. Guy by the name of Luckman. Too bad you didn't stumble over his body, too.'

That was an area of conversation I could live without. Forcing some kind of grin, I said

'Luckman? With an L? No, I'm still working through the H's. Hall was my last one.'

'Shoulda tripped over Luckman,' he insisted. 'A beauty.'

It was almost as if he was tormenting me, but he had no way of knowing that.

'Well, tell it,' I invited, 'or do I have to buy the Sentinel?'

'Nah,' he negatived. 'For you, the courtesies of the trade. Well now, this Luckman. Quite a guy, it seems. Seems to have been into a lot of stuff. Blue movies, for openers. Blackmail, on the side.'

'Sounds like a great loss to the community,' I observed. 'Who killed him, and when does he get a medal for it?'

'There are times, Preston,' he reproved, 'when you display a certain cynicism. It's very unseemly when you speak of those who have passed over. Especially somebody rich. There ought to be more respect when people are rich. Haven't you ever noticed that?'

I thought about the joint on Conquest Street, the unpretentious bungalow out in Pearl Valley. Something here did not jell.

'Rich? A blue movie peddler? I suppose it's possible.'

I managed to carry sufficient doubt into my tone to provoke Hatch into further explanation.

'You're forgetting the blackmail,' he reminded. 'No telling what that might have run to. And no tax to pay. Anyway, wherever he got it, there's no doubt he had it. Man's been buying gold the last few years. I only found out by accident. Just passing the time of day in the newsroom with one of our financial wizards, and I happened to mention Luckman's name. This guy almost jumped on me with excitement. Seems Luckman had been attracting quite some attention in the finance world. Mystery speculator, that kind of stuff.'

'Well, that clears up the mystery,' I suggested. 'The Internal Revenue should have a whale of a time deciding what belongs to who.'

But he was shaking his head.

'You oughta let me finish before you wade in,' he remonstrated. 'The Revenue will have a ball, maybe. First, they have to locate the loot. In other words, whoever bumped off old George seems to have removed the gold at the same time. That was the motive, you see.'

I was in a difficult position. On the one hand, I wanted to pump Tip Hatch until he was dry on the subject of the Luckman murder. On the other hand, I didn't want to arouse his suspicions by seeming too interested. But I had to know more about the gold. This was a whole new area, and it could change everything. The dirty pictures and the blackmail involved only a few people, maybe a dozen at most. This is a workable number, something a man can tackle.

Gold was something else. Gold brought in every con-man, every stick-up artist, every wise guy in the entire State. Beyond the State, I amended. Gold is no respecter of judicial boundaries.

'Just a minute, Tip. You say whoever killed him took the gold. You're not seriously suggesting this Luckman kept the stuff at home? Like, where? Under the bed?'

He thrust out his lower lip, and creases appeared in his forehead.

'Wouldn't know where,' he admitted. 'And it does sound kind of crazy, I have to admit. There's a mystery, all right. Gold isn't like jewellery. You can't just shove it in a strong box and hide the key. It's heavy, and it takes up room. It's early yet to be absolutely positive, but there's no trace of where Luckman was keeping the stuff. All the bank vaults and security firms are being screened right now. Maybe it'll turn up, but the financial people don't think so. Seems there are certain regulations covering the storage of gold, once it gets beyond a certain amount. Anyway, if I sound vague about the details, it's because I'm no expert. Not my subject. But this I'll tell you, subject or no. A guy gets himself bumped off and a whole parcel of gold goes missing, I don't have to be told there's a connection. I know it.'

I knew it, too, though I could have wished I didn't.

9

I called the office to tell Florence Digby that we had a client. She would be only too pleased to record the fact that we were now working for no less a firm than Andrews Clark and Andrews. It gave the place a little status, and she made approving noises as she took down the details.

'You did say Gettysburg?' she queried.

She heard perfectly well what I said. It was just that she wanted to hear it again.

'With a G,' I confirmed. 'Well, that's it. Any messages?'

'Nothing,' she replied. 'Things have been very quiet.'

'I'll be at Parkside for the next hour or so. There's a movie I want to see.'

'Tch, tch,' she tch tched, and we hung up.

It was just the kind of thing she would expect me to do. Sitting at home, watching movies, instead of getting out on the street looking for Angela Stefano. Well, I didn't rate my chances of finding the girl very high, in broad daylight. She would know people would be looking for her by now. Not only the law, and perhaps someone like me, but also the man who killed her — her what? Boy-friend? Abducter? I didn't know what category the late Benny Hall fitted into. Not in relation to Angela. In relation to the rest of the world I had less of a problem. The man had been an all-round rat.

Back at Parkside, I peeled off my sticky clothes and climbed under the shower. Five minutes of the needle spray, and I felt able to face up to the rest of the day. It was time to go to the movies, but not the kind I'd led Florence to believe. There were two epics I'd removed from the stockpile of Still Life Portraits, and there was just a chance I might learn something. I studied the two titles, pondering where to start. 'Under-Age Nympho' carried a faint repulsion, while 'Insatiable Irma' sounded even less appetising. I slotted Nympho into the video and sat down to watch. The picture started with a man pacing up and down in the torture chamber I'd already seen. He was George Luckman, but this time without the floral pajamas. Now he was dressed all in black, with leather belt and shiny riding boots. Insignia on his shoulders left the viewer to assume that he was some kind of interrogator in a totalitarian state. The door opened and another man came in, younger. I realised he was Hall, and it was a strange experience to see these two, whom I had known only in death, whispering to each other.

'What time did you give the girl the drug?' demanded Luckman.

'At four-thirty sir, as you instructed,' replied Hall.

Luckman looked at his watch.

'Then she will be about ready for us. As we are ready for her, eh?'

He nudged Hall, who licked his lips.

'I've been ready all day, sir.'

'That is your trouble,' reproved his commander. 'No sense of timing. Timing is everything in these matters. The girl understands that we can save her father from the firing squad?'

Hall nodded.

'I have told her a dozen times. She knows that if you are pleased with her, you might sign her father's release.'

'Good.'

Luckman laughed into the camera.

'That will add a certain piquancy to the occasion. Particularly since you and I know the fool was executed yesterday morning. Very well, I too am ready for her now.'

Hall went out, leaving the door open. A few seconds later, he was back, half-carrying, half-dragging a girl in a black gym slip and white blouse. Her face was puffy, and the eyes glazed. I had no doubt she was Angela Stefano.

The two men began to shout at her, slapping her around, and tearing at her clothes. They didn't waste much time before tossing her onto a narrow bed. Then they got down to what the customers had paid to see.

It was stomach-churning. After about five minutes, I switched it off. There were still twenty minutes to run, but I'd had all

I could stand. Besides, I'd seen enough. What a pity it was that the last reel didn't show what happened to the two heroes in real life. A few close-ups of their bullet-shattered bodies might have given the raincoat squad something to think about on the way home. At least they were dead, and I was glad of it.

I didn't bother with Insatiable Irma. I told myself it would only be more of the same, but that wasn't the whole explanation. The truth was, I couldn't bear to see any more of that child's tortured face.

A thought struck me.

I'd been watching a film. The two principals were in front of the camera almost the whole time. Surely there had to be another man behind the camera? And surely that was a man I wanted to talk to? Quite excited about this new idea, I called up a man I know in the movie business. After we got through with all the long-time-no-see stuff, I put the question to him.

'Listen, I'm thinking of buying a video camera. Come in useful in my business. You know, scene of the crime and all that stuff. What I'm wondering is, suppose I wanted to be seen myself? Could I set the thing up, and leave it running so's I could get into the picture?'

'Not really,' he denied. 'You'd keep getting out of shot, your distances would be all to hell, a dozen things. You'd get something, but it'd be fifty per cent wasted tape.'

'So I'd need a cameraman?'

'Or another camera. If you set up a second camera at a different angle, you'd get a lot more of yourself. Of course, there'd be a hell of an editing job to do. Could drive you crazy if you're not used to it.'

I asked a few more questions for appearances sake, and broke the connection. I thought I had what I wanted. Luckman had set up not two cameras, but three in the studio. That would be more than enough, in expert hands, to cover all the action within the restrictions of the set. On top of which, the actors knew where the cameras were, and would play to them. So, there was no need for an operator, a third man.

Pity.

The phone rang.

'Preston?'

'Yeah?'

'This is Randall. Better get down to headquarters. Man here I want you to take a look at.'

He didn't even wait to hear my reply. That was the way things were at that moment, between me and the homicide crew. Switching off the video, I took the two cassettes and wandered around, looking for a safe place to store them. In these security-conscious days, a man can't be too careful. The apartment falls a little short on steel doors, combination locks and the like. In the end I settled for the usual spot. Under the bed.

When I climbed up those stairs again to the third floor, Randall and Schultz were both in the office, talking in low tones.

'Ah Preston, glad you could make it. Siddown, siddown.'

Randall was being affable, and that made me suspicious. Schultz and I exchanged nods.

'Always glad to help the authorities,' I announced unctuously.

'That's what we need, the public spirit.'

Randall leaned back, inclining his head at Schultz, who promptly went out.

'Something about a man?' I queried.

'He's on the way,' was the reply. 'Anyway, what's your hurry? I only just got you out of bed, didn't I?'

About to make a retort, I suppressed it. With my present departmental standing, anything I said was liable to be wrong. We sat in silence and waited for Schultz to come back.

When he did, there was another man with him. I looked at him, casually, at first, then with recognition. It was mutual.

'That's him,' exclaimed the newcomer. 'That's the man who followed me to the elevator. I told him — '

' — we know what you say you told him,' cut in Randall. Then, to me, 'Do you recognise this man?'

'Yes, I do,' I confirmed readily. 'He was the man kneeling beside Hall's body when I got there. The one who said he

192

was going to call you people.'

'I did call them,' came the protest. 'How else do you imagine they got there?'

'All right, Mr. Washbourne, calm down. That'll be all for now.'

'You mean I can go? I told you all I know. I don't see why you're keeping me here.'

Randall ignored him, and spoke to Schultz.

'Take Mr. Washbourne to the interrogation room, and get his statement. Then we'll see about letting him go home.'

Schultz ushered the protesting Washbourne out of the room, and closed the door. Randall and I inspected each other.

'You think he did it?' I queried.

The sleepy eyes were giving nothing away.

'Not unless he's capable of swallowing the murder weapon, along with unused cartridges.'

'How'd you manage to pick him up?'

Vast sausage fingers spread out on the desk.

'Oddly enough, with your help. That should make you feel good.'

'My help? How?'

'You gave us a description. Since you were catching the elevator from the same floor, it was a reasonable assumption that your man had been into one of the offices on that floor. We asked around, using the description you gave us, and it came up Washbourne. They call it police work.'

He seemed satisfied with himself, and with reason.

'Very nice work, too,' I conceded. 'And it certainly helps me. But I thought you didn't believe me?'

'What I believe and what I don't believe is my business. Checking out possible leads is departmental business.'

Good for the department, I thought privately.

'What's the tale?' I asked. 'Why did he take off like that? He was only a passer-by, or so he says.'

'That's just it,' explained Randall. 'He shouldn't have been passing by. He wasn't supposed to be in Monkton City at all. He was away on business. Overnight business. His overnight business was a lady who runs a little

194

advertising agency on that very same floor. I don't think Mrs. Washbourne knows about the advertising lady.'

'Ah.' That made the kind of sense I could understand. 'I don't suppose he saw who did it.?'

'No. He wasn't in time for that. But he saw the kid running away. Hall's daughter. Pity we didn't know that earlier.'

So Angela was still the daughter, so far as the police knew. This was dangerous ground for me. I was certainly withholding vital information in not reporting that she was Angela Stefano. It would have come out in the end, and I decided to defer the problem as long as possible.

'He didn't mention that to me.'

'Why should he? You don't have a badge. You don't have any status in this at all. By the way, you'll never guess what happened.'

'Try me,' I suggested.

'We had another phone call. From the mayor's office. Seems somebody's made a mistake. Your name was brought in in error.'

It was as close as I was going to get to an apology.

'Somebody ought to be more careful in future,' I said, in an aggrieved tone. 'Do I take it we're all pals again?'

He half-raised his head. Several of his chins resumed their normal task of acting as his neck.

'Didn't say that,' he corrected. 'But you may take it that your place in the queue for the rack has been moved back a few spaces. You been out to Pearl Valley lately?'

It was typical of him to slide that across, just when I might be off-balance. Luckily I'm always wary in that office.

'Pearl Valley? No. What makes you ask?'

'Oh, nothing really. There was a house out there got broken into last night. Neighbors saw a car outside. Could have been yours.'

'Could it really?' I said with heavy sarcasm. 'Do you have any idea just how many millions of cars there are exactly like mine?'

'Yes I do,' he returned, unmoved. 'But they weren't all driving back into town from the direction of Pearl Valley last night. Yours was. Remember?'

Of course. The prowl-cop who gave the message would automatically report in.

'That highway covers half the state,' I reminded him. 'I was nowhere near Pearl Valley. Anyway, what did I steal? I can't keep track of every little breaking and entering.'

He inclined his head again, and the neck became chins.

'How about a half-million in gold?' he suggested quietly, 'or a whole million maybe. Nobody seems to know for sure.'

I gave a low whistle.

'Not me. I'd be sure to remember that. Are you putting me on? You said it was a house. Now it's a bank vault.'

We had another abrupt change of subject.

'What do you know about George Luckman?'

'The man who got killed today? Nothing. I never heard of him.'

'Who said he got killed?' he rapped out.

'I heard it.'

'Where? No, don't tell me. Down at

Sam's bar, right?'

'Right. That's where the newsguys hang out. They're bound to discuss the news.'

'Are they?' he said tiredly. 'Tell you what, I've been considering having a man stationed in that bar. It would halve my enquiry time. What else did you hear about him?'

I shrugged.

'They said he was a rich man. They seemed to think he might be a little bit crooked. But then, that's what they always say if a guy is rich.'

'A little bit crooked?' he gave a hollow laugh. 'Is that what they're saying down there? We'll have to get some fresh newspapermen in this town. A little bit crooked, yet. Huh. The guy was a walking sewer. I'll be frank with you, Preston. Whoever knocked him off was doing a public service. You know what that guy was into. Among other things? Child prostitution.'

There was a new note in his voice now. A deep bitter loathing. He clearly had difficulty in forcing out words which he found repugnant.

'Nasty,' I breathed.

'Know who the kid was?'

'Me? No.'

'It was Hall's daughter, that's who. And your friend Hall, or I should say Halsetti, he was a partner.'

I was having my usual difficulty in trying to remember how much I was supposed to know, as opposed to how much I really knew. The key-note for the moment seemed to be incredulity.

'His own daughter? Aw come on, that's pretty hard to take.'

'Yes it is,' he agreed solemnly. 'But the evidence is incontestable. There are photographs. They're not very pretty. Why on earth am I telling you all this?'

I'd been wondering the same thing.

'I don't know,' I admitted. 'It is a little unusual.'

'Unusual,' he repeated. 'Yes, you could call it that. I am talking to you off the record, and that's how it will stay. You see I have this feeling that you have a hand somewhere in this game. No, don't start in with all the innocent patter, I'm not interested. I'm not saying you were involved at the start. Falling across Halsetti's body that way, it could have been no more than what you said it was. A coincidence. But you've been cropping up ever since. You went to the apartment, you slugged the manager. Don't contradict me, I'm not through. There was a car like yours ourside the Luckman house last night. You were out in that direction. Political people tell us to lay off you, then they tell us they made a mistake. And there's another thing.'

He paused, as if to be sure I was paying attention. That was one thing he need not have been concerned about. My ears must have been twice their normal size.

'Luckman ran a photographic studio down on Conquest Street. That's where he was killed. The scene of crime squad ran over it, and they came up with a half-thumb print. That half-thumb matches your half-thumb, left hand.'

'A half-thumb?' I echoed. 'A fifty per center? Now come on, that's about as useless as no print at all. If you're going to start convicting on halfprints, you may as well abandon the system. You know as well as I do that half the people in the world share fifty per cent of fingerprint characteristics.'

The huge head rolled definitely side-wise.

'Not so. The percentage of similarities goes down with every whorl. Once you get enough to form half the finished article, you are down to — I forget the exact figure, but it's something like fourteen per cent. Did you know that? I didn't know that.'

I was busy trying to do sums in my head.

'Oh great,' I said grimly. 'Fourteen per cent. That means you have a half-print which I share with one in seven of the population. You wouldn't be forgetting the other six, would you?'

'No,' he agreed magnanimously. 'As evidence it's useless. There isn't a court anywhere that would accept it. But we're not talking here about courtrooms. We're talking about me, and my old copper's feeling. When a man's been a cop as long as me, he develops an instinct. A feel for a case. Mine tells me you're in this. I don't know why, and I don't much care. I just feel you're involved. So here's the message. I don't want any big front-page stuff from you. None of your Robin Hood routine. If you get something, I want it. And keep that damned gun locked in a drawer. I don't want a lot of holes made in the guy who rubbed out these two. I want him for trial, and in one piece. And, before I lock him up, I want to shake his hand. For my money, he's with the good guys. Are you getting all this?'

I wagged my head vigorously, all open-faced.

'If anything comes my way, you can rely on me.'

'No I can't,' he contradicted. 'That's what bothers me. If I really wanted any peace of mind, I'd have you locked up, at least until this is over. Ask me why I'm not going to do it.'

'All right, why?' I asked dutifully.

'I'm not going to do it, because I think you may be more use to me out there, than sitting in a cell eating the taxpayer's money. You can do things a public servant can't. You can punch heads, threaten people, and sometimes those things produce answers. Answers are very much in demand at this time. But no grandstanding. Whatever you get, I get. Kabish?'

'Got it. Say, tell me, this million in gold. That was just for a laugh, huh? I mean, nobody has a million in gold.'

'The tale is that Luckman had. Or close to it. If you think it's a fairy tale, take a ride out to his house. You'll find a couple of men there, tearing the place apart looking for it.'

I thought of an immediate objection to that.

'But surely, if those two were murdered because of the gold, the man who killed them will have it.'

His look was almost of pity.

'We're not thinking too well today, are we? That stuff weighs. You don't just shove it in your pocket and walk out. You don't even put it in the back of the car. You need a truck for that quantity. A truck, plus darkness.'

I didn't have to feign innocence for that one.

'Darkness? Why? Does it fade in daylight?'

'Ha ha,' he ha-haed. 'No, it doesn't fade. What we're talking about here is a removal job. One man, working alone, would have to make a lot of trips to carry that much stuff into a truck. And as many more, to unload at the other end. Daylight is out. Passers by, neighbors, anybody who happens to be around. They won't take any notice of a man putting something into a truck. Why should they? It happens all the time. But when a man makes five trips, ten, maybe thirty depending on how the gold is broken down, people will certainly notice. They'll wonder what he's doing. They'll look at him. And that is the last thing our killer wants, is people looking at him. No. He needs the night hours.'

'Didn't he have all last night?' I queried.

'Yes, he did,' agreed Randall, 'but if the gold was at the house in Pearl Valley, I don't think he moved it last night. The local people were quick enough to remember one strange car, once we banged on a few doors. They wouldn't be likely to have overlooked a truck.'

'Then the chances are your men will find it, and our unknown friend will have been wasting his time,' I suggested helpfully.

'I hope so. Lord, I hope so.'

Neither of us referred to the other possibilities. There were too many of them, and I wasn't there to poke holes in Randall's theory. For one thing the gold didn't have to be at the house at all. It could be anywhere. If it existed. That was another, far more likely possibility, that Luckman didn't hang on to it. He could have been taking a trip down to Mexico or some place, every time he made a purchase. Gold is welcome everywhere you go, and the owner along with it. Luckman could have been setting himself up gradually, for an eventual disappearance to a new, wealthy life, whereabouts unknown.

Those things would have occurred to Randall, I knew. I also knew he didn't choose to think about them, and I was far too concerned about my own freedom to want to upset him.

I decided this was the moment for a piece of my open manliness.

'There is one little thing. I didn't bother to mention it before, but since you're so interested in every detail — '

I left it dangling, and he swallowed it up.

'Don't be coy,' he invited. 'Little details are my life's work. What do you have, the killer's name and address?'

'No,' I admitted, 'not quite. There are two Halsetti soldiers in town. They threatened me, waved their popguns at me. You know, the usual stuff.'

'Why would they do that?' he asked gently. 'Considering you don't know anything?'

'It was that damned newscast again,' I grumbled. 'There oughta be some kind of law to protect the innocent from unspoken slander.'

'Unspoken slander?' he repeated. 'Well, I'd have to ask the lawyers about that one. Tell me about the nasty men.'

'Not a lot to tell. They just made noises, like I say, and went away.'

'Why are you telling me?'

'Because they just might find this murderer you're looking for. If they do, they'll deal with it their own way. That wouldn't seem to suit your book.'

He shifted papers around.

'Could you describe these two gentlemen?'

'Sure.'

I gave him what I could recall about Front-Seat and Back-Seat. He didn't attempt to write anything down, but sat with clenched hands during my recital.'

'Very good,' he intoned, like some schoolteacher. 'Would they be anything like this?'

He tossed over a photograph, and I picked it up. My two friends from the rear of the Globe building stared glumly at the camera.

'That's them,' I admitted with surprise. 'What'd they do?'

'Do? They didn't do anything.' Randall was enjoying himself. 'A patrol car down in the Fourth Precinct saw two strangers around the old home town. The kind of strangers we can live without. So they ran the rule over the visitors, and it turned out they were just what you said. Two strong arm guys from upstate, well known to our brethren in the S.F.P.D. So they tossed 'em in the can. It's called police work. We do it all the time.'

It was a comfort, with so many people breathing over my shoulder, to know that two of the breathers were temporarily off duty.

'What'll be the charge?' I asked.

'There'll be no charge,' he replied. 'The precinct people will just make unfriendly noises, and put these comedians on a train. They won't be coming back. Should make you feel better.'

'It does,' and I meant it. 'Well, if you're about through with me — ?'

He took a long time about replying.

'Through? No, I wouldn't put it quite that way. Let's say rather, I don't need you any more at the moment.'

I wasted no time in getting to my feet.

'What'll happen to Mr. Washbourne?'

For the first time he showed genuine amusement.

'I'd say that was rather up to Mrs.

Washbourne. Wouldn't you?'

It's a funny thing, how we can always find something to laugh at in other people's misfortunes.

Maybe there was something funny about mine.

I just couldn't see it.

10

Somebody had been inside my car. The doors were still locked, but when I got behind the wheel I found an envelope taped to it. I was more anxious than annoyed. At least they locked the door behind them. Precaution against the crime element, I reflected sourly, as I ripped open the envelope.

Inside was a large coarse Treasury note. The part that mattered read One Thousand Dollars. With it was a piece of white paper, with words scrawled on it. They said 'Go home and wait'. There was no signature, no address. There didn't have to be. My circle of acquaintances is wide, but it narrows sharply when you get down to the people who leave terse orders around, along with thousand dollar bills. This was a communique from my head office, from the chairman of the board himself. Mr. Harrison Page was in touch with his field operative.

I sat there, fretting and feeling power-less. A man doesn't like to be jerked around like a puppet on a string, and that was exactly the way Page treated me. I stared out of the car window. There were people all over the place, cars galore. Any of them could belong to Page. Any of them could be watching me, just to see what I did next. They needn't have worried. I was going to do exactly what I was told. Page said so, and the money confirmed it.

I drove slowly back to Parkside, keeping my eyes peeled for strangers all the way to the door of my apartment. Nobody seemed to take any notice of me. When I got in, the telephone rang at once.

I picked it up.

'Yup?'

Page's voice said

'We won't bother with names, but you know who this is.'

'Yes I do,' I confirmed.

'Good. Did you receive my — er — letter?'

'I did. That's why I'm here.'

'Kay. Now listen to this, and don't get it wrong. Someone is coming to see you. He'll be there in one hour. You wait for him, and you listen to him. He speaks for me. You understand that? He speaks for me.'

'Got it.'

'Good. We won't be talking again.'

He hung up on me before I could say anything else. Thoughtfully I replaced the receiver. What did it mean? The answer seemed clear. First, the money, then Page telling me goodbye. It looked as if I was off the case. But if so, why was I going to have a visitor? And why cut me out, anyway? The killer hadn't been found yet. Or had he? Perhaps some of Page's goons had turned him up, and they didn't need me any more. Perhaps — oh this was ridiculous. I was piling one speculation on top of another, and winding up with speculations.

The facts were simple.

Page had taken me off the case. Someone was coming to talk to me. I had an extra thousand dollars. In those circumstances, a man doesn't sit around

212

speculating. He tucks the money away and treats himself to a shower and a change of laundry. Then he pours himself a light measure of Uncle Jock and puts plenty of ice in, and parks himself in front of the tee vee to wait for his visitor.

There was a newscast on. I watched a detachment of marines marching into some tropical state on a peace mission, then it switched to a local scene. George Luckman made the first item. They showed pictures of the studio on Conquest Street, and the bungalow out at Pearl Valley. There was no mention of blue movies or blackmail, but gold was featured. To listen to the man behind the microphone, you'd have pegged Luckman as some kind of finance whizz kid. They played up the missing bullion angle, and I had a vision of half the population setting out on another gold chase, only this time it would be the neighbors' back yard they were digging up. Luckman didn't seem to have any family, at least none that had been traced this far, and so ownership of the gold seemed to be up for grabs. The station did a good job in the lip-licking department. It wouldn't be their fault if the whole area didn't go gold crazy in the next twenty-four hours. This conjured up some fanciful images in my mind. Maybe, after a few hectic days, Washington might find themselves sending in some more marines, only this time the peace mission would be to Monkton City.

After the high excitement of the new forty-nine, the reference to Benny Hall's murder came as an anticlimax.

' — and still no developments have been reported. But the police would like you to take a close look at this picture. Have you see this little girl?'

And on the screen came Angela Stefano. It was the girl from the cot pictures I'd seen at the Luckman house. But now she was different. Now she was everybody's favorite kid sister. A happy smiling young face, with shining hair brushed away from tiny ears. She wore a tee shirt with crazy badges pinned all over the place, and you could see a dozen like her down any Main Street, any day.

I stared at her sadly, and yet with relief. This was the way she ought to look, the way people ought to think of her. She was nothing to me, and yet I felt somehow responsible. Certainly I didn't want Joe Public looking at that face the way I'd seen it, twisted with suffering and shame. I wondered where the police had found the photograph. Perhaps the parents — no, that couldn't be it. The police didn't yet know about that angle. That, so far, was between Mr. Andrews and me. Well, it was just a picture, no, it wasn't. There was something about the background, something familiar. I squinted hard at the screen. The photograph had been taken inside the Luckman house at Pearl Valley. There could be no mistake, because I could make out that weird art decor heap of rocks behind her in the window.

So that must mean that at some stage, Angela had felt quite relaxed and easy in Luckman's presence. Perhaps he'd even been good old Uncle George for a while. She wouldn't have known then about what was waiting for her on Conquest Street. I could feel myself getting angry all over again, and knew I was going to have to cut it out. In my job, a man can't afford too much by way of personal involvement. Anyway it was a futile kind of anger. The two people it was directed against were both dead, and good riddance. Randall had been right. Whoever bumped off those two characters was performing a public service. I, for one, would lose no sleep if he got away with it. Maybe I'd been saved by the bell. Maybe Harrison Page was cutting me out at just the right time.

As if on cue, the door-buzzer blattered away.

I peeked through the spy-hole, to see a well-dressed man about my own age staring confidently back at me. Sliding bolts I opened the door.

'Mr. Preston? I believe you're expecting me.'

He made no move to come inside until I asked him. It gave an indication of how things were to be conducted. Smooth, well-mannered. It had the authentic Page feel about it.

I got him parked in a club chair. He refused to smoke, but joined me in a spot of Uncle Jock — 'very weak please' — and then we sat, looking at each other. He didn't offer any name.

'This is a nice place you have Mr. Preston.'

'Mr' yet.

'This job brings bruises,' I told him. 'I like to nurse them in comfort.'

'And why not?'

He tipped his glass towards me and took a small sip.

'You didn't tell me who you are?' I reminded him.

That brought me a shrug from well-clothed shoulders.

'Barclay,' he replied. 'Call me Barclay.'

I squinted at him suspiciously.

He smiled, letting me see that all his dental bills were paid up.

'It's a name I've always liked. Has a kind of ring to it, don't you think?'

It was all I was going to get. I grinned. You couldn't help liking the man, Barclay or no.

'Well O.K. Mr. Barclay, you seem to have the floor. I gather my services are no longer required. Are you going to tell me why?'

He nodded, setting the scarcely-touched drink down beside him.

'Yes, I am. My principal wants you to understand that he has no fault to find with you. None whatever. I think your — um — severence pay makes that quite clear?'

'Very satisfactory,' I assured him. 'Generous.'

'Good, good. Well, as I say, there is no criticism of you. It is simply that things have changed.'

'Changed how?' I challenged.

He rested his arms easily along the arms of the chair, and sat back.

'This started out as a simple matter,' he declaimed. 'A question of business good will. A gesture, if you like, to certain interested persons in San Francisco. My principal had nothing to gain but what he did. He simply extended the hand of friendship.'

'That's how he explained it to me,' I assented.

His nod was emphatic.

'Of course he did. Of course. That's all it was. Then.'

'So what's different now? Did Mr. — ' I stopped at the slightly alarmed expression on his face. ' — I should say, your principal, did he get mad because of those two guns the Halsettis sent down here?'

'Oh dear me no,' he denied. 'No, that was just a gut-reaction from the lower orders. Almost to be expected, really. No, what has made the difference has been the death of this Luckman person. The story is, and there is truth in it, that a large quantity of gold is missing.'

It was my turn to sit back and relax. After all, it is my place.

'A million dollars worth, so they say.'

He gave a rueful smile.

'So they say. But then, they always do, don't they? Anything less fails to grip the public imagination. No. Our information is that the total is rather less. Probably a little over half-a-million. But we are not the public, Mr. Preston. Our imagination is quite sufficiently gripped by half-a-million. Particularly in gold. Gold is currency anyplace in the world, and very few people really care where it comes from.'

I took a good pull at the Uncle Jock.

'So, if I understand you, what we have here is a shift of emphasis. Would that be the expression? I think it would. The good will, the hand of friendship, all that stuff goes out the window then the bullion comes centre-stage?'

His eyes twinkled while he digested it.

'You have a certain direct way of speaking Mr. Preston, which is probably not always popular.'

'Not always,' I agreed. 'But tell me if I'm wrong.'

A shaft of sunlight struck a low blush from his cufflinks. Silver would have gleamed. The blush made them platinum. I'll say one thing for Harrison Page. He didn't send cheap messengers.

'Let me put it this way. When you had your little discussion with my principal, I think he made himself perfectly clear. In fact, knowing him, I'm sure of it. Everything was to be out in the open. A proper arrest, a proper trial, a conviction. Plenty of publicity. You'll correct me if I get anything wrong?'

'You're doing fine,' I assured him.

'Splendid. Well now, you can see how the gold upsets things. The fact is, Mr. Preston, we want it. We intend to have it. That lets you out.'

I looked all innocent.

'Why?'

'Now now,' he said reprovingly. 'It's obvious enough. The very reason you were given this job is the same one that now disqualifies you. Basically you are an honest man. I don't mean to imply that you are gullible, or too wide-eyed. You're not above diverting a few dollars to your own use, if the opportunity arises. Take this gold, for example. If you found it, what would you do? I think I can answer my own question. Everything would depend on the circumstances, naturally. But, if they gave you the chance, you would probably put a small proportion of it on one side for a rainy day. You would regard that as no more than your right. A finder's charge, a tax-free benefit. But the rest you would hand over to the proper authorities. That is the way you operate.

In fact, that is largely why the state keeps on renewing your licence. Admirable. I mean it. But for our own purposes, it makes you unsuitable.'

I couldn't fault his reasoning. For a moment there, I had considered butting in, when he said I might salt a little of the bullion away. That didn't fit in too well with my Honest Joe portrayal, but the objection died inside my head, before it was properly formulated. What would I really do, if I found myself alone with all that loot? I didn't know, not for sure, but I suspected that Barclay's version would be close to the truth.

'So you're taking me off the case,' I muttered.

'You are already off,' he corrected. 'As of now. I think you would agree the terms as generous?'

'Easiest two grand I ever collected,' I admitted. 'Pity though. I was just getting interested.'

'A pity, indeed, but there it is.'

He started to rise from the chair, but I held up a hand.

'Just a moment Mr. Barclay, there's

something else you ought to know.'

Surprised, he settled back.

'Go on,' he invited.

'I'm still looking for the girl. Little Angela.'

Faint frown lines appeared above his nose.

'Halsetti's daughter? Oh, I don't think we like that very much. Are you proposing to tell me why?'

'For one thing, she isn't Halsetti's daughter,' I told him, watching his face. If he already knew, he gave no sign. 'She's a high-school kid who ran away with Halsetti, or got dragged away. I'm not sure of the truth.'

The frown-lines were now furrowed.

'But are you sure of what you're telling me?'

'Absolutely.'

He sat forward, drumming well-manicured fingers on his knee.

'This is certainly a complication. Do you intend to tell me how you know?'

I'd been wondering the same thing, but there seemed no harm in it.

'Why not?' I returned expansively. 'The

girl's parents hired me to find her.'

'Oh dear.' He lowered his eyebrows. 'I don't think I like that too well. You already had a client. A client who was paying handsomely for your services. It doesn't sound very ethical for you to be working for two different people on the same case.'

It was a question, and he was waiting for me to answer it.

'You're absolutely right, and ordinarily I wouldn't have touched it. But think it through, Mr. Barclay. Let me tell you how I weighed it up, and you can decide whether I made the wrong choice.'

He nodded, looking serious.

'You will certainly have my full attention.'

'The girl's parents want her found privately. No cops, no newspapers. They just wanted their daughter back, and the whole thing hushed up. Plenty of parents would feel the same way.'

I looked across to see if he wanted to argue, but he merely inclined his head.

'The only way for them to do that was

to hire somebody private. My name was already being splashed around, and so I got the job. My first reaction was to refuse. I was already working for Mr. — for your boss. But then I thought a second time. If I turned them down, would they drop it? The answer was a large 'No'. They would go somewhere else. There's plenty of people in my line of work. Too many.' That was by way of being a grouch and a joke at the same time. The audience reaction was nil, on both counts. 'That would involve some-body else taking a hand in the game. Somebody else poking around, asking questions, stirring things up. Such a person might upset everything, do it all wrong. Do things the way your boss did not want, come up with the wrong solution. I decided we were all better off if this thing was kept in the family. That's why I accepted the assignment. Now, tell me where I was wrong.'

'H'm.'

He leaned back in the chair, tilting his head towards the ceiling, with closed eyes.

'I can see where you were placed in a very difficult position. I must say, this news about the girl comes as something of a surprise. You must forgive me if I think out loud, but I'm wondering why our friends in San Francisco failed to make this point clear to us.'

If I had any opinion about that, I certainly was going to keep it to myself. If the big hoodlums up there started to fall out with the big ditto around my territory, I did not wish to be among those present.

'Well, no matter,' he decided. 'That's another subject. The immediate question is, what do you do now? And the answer is, you drop it.'

'No.'

I tried to say it without a lot of emphasis, but it came out loud and clear.

Barclay looked startled, then curious.

'Now that my principal has dropped out, there is no necessity for you to continue this charade with these other people. If it's a question of returning their fee, we might be able to — '

'It isn't the fee,' I interrupted.

Now he was frankly puzzled.

'What then?'

'It's the girl. I want to see her. I want to know that she's all right.'

Barclay's look was frankly sceptical.

'You don't strike me as the parental type,' he said coldly.

It was clear he did not believe me, and thought I was holding out on him.

'This Luckman was into dirty pictures, did you know that? Not looking at them. Making them.'

'So?'

'So this kid was involved. I've seen some of the stuff they did to her. Let me tell you, if either of those two jokers was still alive, I'd think very hard about bumping them off myself.'

'And that's your only reason? It doesn't sound very strong,' he objected.

'It would seem stronger if you'd seen what I saw,' I told him obstinately.

Seeing that there was no point in further argument, he got to his feet.

'Those pictures must have been pretty raw,' he said, watching my face.

'Raw is right.'

He hesitated fractionally, then said

'You realise the chances are very strong that the girl is dead?'

The thought had crossed my mind more than once, but I refused to have anything to do with it.

'I don't think so.'

Barclay shrugged.

'I'd think about it again. Whoever is after that money means business. The girl is probably a witness to her — to Halsetti's shooting. She was seen running away just after it happened.'

'How'd you know that? The police only found out a few hours ago.'

He gave a self-satisfied chuckle.

'You'll forgive me if I protect my sources. Anyway, the fact remains that she is or was a danger to the man we want. I think he's probably dealt with that problem. If not, why hasn't she turned up? Or why hasn't somebody reported her? Face the facts, man.'

But I didn't choose to face the facts. Not his facts. I liked my facts better. Mine had Angela Stefano alive and well.

At the door he paused.

'If you persist in going on with this, you realise you might come to a situation where your interests and ours are in conflict?'

It sounded a routine question. Casual, almost. But I know a death-warning when I heard one.

'I'll try to keep out of your way,' I assured him.

'That would be very sensible,' he smiled, and was gone.

I stared at the closed door.

Sensible?

In the last couple of days, I had collected two and a half thousand dollars on this case. That was nice money by any reckoning. What a sensible man would do, he'd hurry out to the track, and try turning two and a half thousand into two and a half million. Or he'd jump on a plane to Vegas, objective similar. He might even hire a long sleek boat, find a long sleek blonde, and pretend to go fishing for a few days.

That's what a sensible man would do.

Looking back on it, I wish I had.

11

I'd never had a great deal of personal contact with gold, not real gold.

Money, yes. Money was an old acquaintance, and where there was trouble, particularly my kind of trouble, money usually figured in the background sooner or later. I understand money. You can hold it in your hand, put it in your pocket. With money, you can buy things. Cigarets, corporations, people. You can buy anything and almost anybody, if you can produce enough of that good green folding paper. But it doesn't have any connection with gold. Gold is something for the government. They make bricks out of it, and lock it up in a fortress in the desert, where nobody else can touch it or even see it. Money is the little currency, but gold is the big one. With gold you can start your own war, or buy a country. It is a dull yellowish metal, unattractive to look at, and carrying with it the very seeds of corruption. Right down the ages, gold has left in its wake a terrible record of carnage, deceit and large scale disaster. I'm no historian, but I don't recall a single instance where gold gets the credit for saving a country, curing a plague, or indeed doing one single damned thing which was of any benefit to anybody. Maybe that's why they lock it up in the desert, where it can't do anyone any harm.

But they didn't have it all, not yet.

There were little odd parcels of it scattered around, still causing trouble, still in the death and destruction business. It was just my bad luck to have one of those parcels come my way, with the usual and inevitable results. I had no doubt about one thing. As long as that bullion remained undiscovered, there could only be more mayhem. And from now on, it could come from any direction. The new forty-niners would be homing in on Monkton City in droves. But these men were different. They wouldn't be bringing picks and shovels and shifting pans. They would bring guns and automobiles and organisation. They would not be interested in who killed who, or whatever had become of little Angela Stefano. Their sole interest would be in finding the gold, and latching on to it.

If I could somehow remove the gold element from this case, then all these outside interests would melt away, and I could get on with what I had to do. At the back of my mind was an idea. True enough, it was probably crazy, but it wouldn't go away. I felt the need of some company, before I could test out my theory, and I sat by the phone sending out signals for Sam Thompson. I'd already called five places without result, leaving messages everywhere for him to call back, and I was looking up the number of one more side-street bar when the phone blatted.

Thompson had been quick. I picked it up gladly.

'Sam?'

A strange voice said

'Huh? Is that you, Preston?'

Disappointed I replied

'Yes, this is Preston. Who'm I talking to?'

'This is Gabe Milton.'

Gabe Milton? I couldn't recall the name, but there was something familiar about the voice.

'Do I know you?' I queried.

'I would hope,' he replied sourly. 'You got me plastered last time you was here. The Almira Apartments. Remember?'

The manager, of course.

'Sure, I remember. What can I do for you, Gabe?'

'Listen,' and suddenly he was whispering. 'There's going to be some kind of reward, ain't there? I mean, with all that gold and all.'

'Could be, Gabe,' I hedged. 'Do you know where it is?'

He became crafty then.

'Ah well now, that'd be telling, huh? But, about the reward — '

'I wouldn't know. Nothing's been announced so far. If you want me to get in touch with people — '

'No wait. I got a better idea. Jesus.'

He didn't get to tell me what the better

idea was. There were two loud explosions, then a high-pitched female scream. A third explosion, then a series of muffled thumps and thuds I couldn't identify. By now, I was shouting into the mouthpiece.

'Gabe, what's going on? Hey, are you there? Is anyone there?'

There were no sounds now at the other end. I stared at the receiver, feeling impotent. Willing it to let me see down the cable and out the other end. Reluctantly I put it back on the cradle. Some people might have thought those sharp noises came from a back-firing car, but I knew better. Somebody had been shooting off a gun, and I had better get down to the Almira as fast as I could shift. Guns call for guns, and I made myself pause long enough to check the thirty eight before I stuck it in my waistband.

Then I steeled myself not to run to the car, but it called for effort. The feminine scream kept echoing in my head. It couldn't possibly have been Angela Stefano. Why would she be with the

Almira manager? It didn't make any sense. On the other hand, why not? She had to be somewhere.

I don't remember the drive at all. I must have stopped at crossings, threaded my way through the cross-town traffic, just like everyone else. But it was automatic. My mind was not present. It was way off, ranging over one speculation after another, turning over every remote hypothesis, accepting or discarding crazy notions by the dozen.

But I can remember parking the car, and locking it. The sun was dropping now, and welcome squares and oblongs of cool shadow were beginning to spread over the concrete. People were coming and going about their affairs, just as though nothing had happened. I don't know what I'd expected to find. An ambulance outside the building, a couple of prowl-cars with the rotating orange flashers proclaiming some kind of nearby disaster. Something. But there was nothing.

In my haste, I forgot that the main entrance door didn't work properly and I wasted valuable seconds before remembering about the smaller door. Inside, there was silence. I fingered at the hard metal against my middle for reassurance, then walked over to the manager's apartment. The door stood slightly open. Reason, calm reason told me there would not be anyone waiting inside. Waiting for me, anybody. The hell with calm reason, it was my neck that was on the line.

I slid out the gun, pressed myself against the wall, and reached around to push the door wide. Nothing happened. Then I ducked down to a crouch, took a deep breath, and went in, low and fast.

The place was a shambles. There was furniture lying on its side, stuff scattered all over the floor. Somebody had put up a fight in here, and it hadn't been Gabe Milton. He was lying face down on the floor, in front of the television cabinet. There was no one else in the room. Standing up, I checked the rest of the place, still half-expecting an ambush. I didn't have much to cover. There was a small kitchen, empty, and a bedroom, ditto.

I went back into the main room, then realised I was standing around with a gun in my hand, a dead body on the floor, and the other door wide open. Crossing the room quickly, I closed the door and put the gun away. The situation called for privacy.

Staring down at Milton's body, I could see no signs of damage. Bending over, I muttered an apology, and turned him over. He was a big man, and it took quite an effort to shift him. There was a huge bloodstain all across his middle, with two darker stains where the slugs had gone in. I had heard a third shot, and if it hadn't been fired at Milton, it must mean — no, it mustn't. I didn't want to think about that possibility, and anyway, it was probably wrong. There had been no more screaming after the third shot. That was true. But, on the other hand if Angela, no not Angela, if the woman who screamed had been killed, why bother to remove the body? It made no sense.

I rolled Milton back into position. The phone. I remembered that the phone had been off the hook when it all happened.

Somebody had put it back. Apart from the general disorder, there was nothing for me to learn in this room. I hadn't yet looked at the bedroom properly, other than to satisfy myself there was no one lurking in there.

Stepping inside, I knew Angela had been there. There were pieces of teenage clothing all over the place, and it had to be her. On the other side of the bed I found a tee shirt lying on the floor. Picking it up, I found there was blood on it. Fresh blood, high on the left shoulder. Too high for the heart, I told myself thankfully. I felt very close to her in that room, really close for the first time. Sitting on the bed, I lit an Old Favorite and stared around, trying to get things in focus. There was one fact I couldn't get away from. The apartment contained only one bed, and there was no sign of a shakedown on the couch in the other room. That could mean only one thing. Angela had been paying for her shelter in the one way she knew, the way that must have become so sickeningly familiar to her.

No wonder the police couldn't find her. No wonder some member of the public hadn't reported seeing her around. The answer was right here. Angela had never left the building. She had probably been here in the bedroom when I was pouring whisky down Milton in the outer room. Why hadn't she come out? Why hadn't she even called to me? I wouldn't have hurt her. I would have looked after her. She wouldn't have had to let that fat slob outside paw at her, there would have been no need for any of this. He might even still be alive. So why didn't she let me know she was there?

But of course I knew the answer, even as I asked the question.

To her I was just another male voice, another source of potential pain and misery. That was all she had come to expect from men, ever since she came to this city. Halsetti, Luckman, Luckman's swinish customers, Milton. Why should I be any different? No, she wasn't going to trust herself to me, and I couldn't blame her. I fingered at the bloody tee shirt. Who had taken her now, and why? Not for ransom, and not as a hostage. What then. It had to be one of two things. Either Angela knew where the gold was hidden, or the kidnappers merely thought she did. That gave her a breathing space, either way. They had to keep her alive until she led them to the gold, or until they finally realised she didn't know where it was. Then — but I wasn't going to think about that.

I took one final look around the apartment, without any clear idea of what I expected to find. There was nothing unusual. Nothing to give any lead as to who the intruders might have been. Satisfied that there was nothing to be gained by further delay, I went out, pulling the door closed behind me. Then I drove a couple of blocks away, and pulled in to think.

One thing was clear. I wasn't going to achieve anything until I got my mind free of Angela Stefano. All the guesswork, all the speculation in the world was not going to help her in the slightest. Nor me. I know my own make-up in situations like this. What I was liable to do, was to work myself up into a rage of frustration. Then I would erupt. I would go out and do something violent or foolish. Or, more likely, a combination of the two. Nobody would gain, and I'd wind up in some kind of trouble. I'd done it often enough in the past, before I finally reasoned out a solution.

The solution is simple. If there is nothing useful to be done in one direction, then you find something positive to do in another, and you do it. You don't do it half-heartedly, but with full concentration. Otherwise the point is lost.

Before Gabe Milton made his fatal telephone call, I'd been about to test a wildcat theory. It was a hundred to one shot, but that was better than no odds at all. Plus, it was something to do. I would go through with it, I decided, and began searching for change for the telephone. The first thing was to locate Sam Thompson.

* * *

It was nearly full dark when I reached Pearl Valley. Lights were on in most of the houses, as people settled in for the evening after the day's work. It was quiet out there, quiet and peaceful as I drove down toward's Luckman's house. I was gambling that the police would have given up by now, and left. There were a number of cars parked both sides of the street, but none of them looked official. The road outside the Luckman place was empty, and there were no lights from inside. Remembering the way the nosey neighbors had reported my car after my previous visit, I left it fifty yards up the street, under a clump of trees. Then I walked slowly back. I didn't see what harm I could come to in an empty house, but I was still reassured by the ready availability of my Police Special.

The front door was firmly locked, but I went around the side and found that one of the rear doors had been forced, then made secure by a couple of wooden slats, nailed across. It only took one heave for one of the slats to come away in my hand, and then I was inside. I'd brought a pencil torch from the car, and the narrow beam picked its way around the interior.

There were signs everywhere of the police search. Even the floorboards had been prised up, and banged into position. If Luckman had any heirs, I reflected, somebody was going to get sued.

The temptation to switch the light on was great, but I didn't feel I could risk it. Gil Randall hadn't bothered to press too hard about my first trip to the house, but he wouldn't be prepared to accept any cock-and-bull story a second time.

The ugly rock-pile was still in place in front of the window. Moving gently across the room, I stood and stared at it in the dying daylight. It made no more sense now than the last time I saw it. It was just as formless, just as ugly, just as haphazard. To an untutored eye that is. For a more informed view, I would have had to consult those sickly kids with wispy beards who sit around on the library steps, complaining about the government.

But they weren't here. They weren't standing in that silent, dark house, with its dusty smell caused by the police disturbances. If they had been, they would probably have tried to prevent the sacrilege I was about to inflict on this work of art.

Reaching the table, I ran my fingers over the black rock, feeling the contours, the planes and slopes. It didn't tell me anything, except that shiny paint makes for a slippery surface. I found a couple of books, and wedged the torch so that light played on the sculpture. Then I took out a clasp knife and opened it. Picking a spot in the direct beam of the light, I began to scrape gently at the paint. Small black flakes crumbled away, and I blew them clear. There was more paint underneath. Harder now, I went to work again with the knife. The paint must have had a rubber base or something. It certainly did not wish to leave that surface. A scratch appeared in the black, then another. Furiously now, I pressed against the blade, willing the paint to go away. Suddenly a large flake came away in one piece, about an inch square. Not fully believing what I thought I saw, I picked up the torch, and played it fully on the exposed rock.

The rock was yellow.

I was leaning on half-a-million dollars worth of gold.

The sudden flooding of the room with light was an anti-climax.

A small voice said

'Who are you? What are you doing here?'

I turned around slowly, to get my first real look at Angela Stefano.

12

She looked even younger than the
photographs. The rich black hair was
caught up at each side with a bowed
ribbon. Wide eyes inspected me gravely
from a serene, unlined face. She wore a
tailored white blouse and a red dirndl
skirt. Everything about her said gradua-
tion day. Everything except the ugly
short-snouted revolver which she held,
pointed firmly at my chest.

'Well?' she demanded.

I held out a hand, palm forward.

'You can put that down, Angela. You're
in no danger from me.'

A frown flitted across the smooth
forehead, and vanished as quickly as it
came.

'Angela? You know my name?'

But the gun did not waver.

'Yes,' I said gently. 'My name is
Preston. I'm a — '

'Ah,' she interrupted. 'Preston. You're a

lot younger than I imagined. How did you know I'd be here?'

There was something wrong with this conversation, but at that moment I couldn't identify what it was.

'I didn't,' I admitted. 'I came out for another reason. But I'm glad I found you. Everything is going to be fine, now. I can get you back to your parents and — '

'My who?'

There was incredulity in her words, and it reflected in her eyes.

'Your parents,' I repeated. 'They contacted a firm of lawyers here in town, and they hired me to find you. I wish you'd put that gun down. It might go off.'

'Yes, it might,' she agreed. 'That's why it stays where it is. What is this shit about parents? Who'm I supposed to be?'

The casual use of the bad language had a shocking effect, coming from that young face. For the first time I began to feel uneasy. My light laugh came out slightly cracked.

'I know all about what happened back home, but believe me, things are all right with your family. They just want you back.'

She stared at me unwaveringly, digesting this.

'Tell me about these parents,' she invited. 'What name did they give?'

Feeling rather foolish, I told her what her name was.

'Why, Stefano of course.'

'Ah.'

It was more of a hiss than an exclamation.

'So they know it's me.'

It was almost as though she was talking to herself. Then she waggled the gun, in a gesture of command.

'Sit down. In that chair there.'

I went without argument, and sat. This girl was in a state of high tension, and it wouldn't take a lot to make her squeeze the trigger.

Her body relaxed slightly once I was safely seated, but the gun was as stiff as ever. Then she gave me a wry grin.

'Tell me the truth,' she commanded. 'Are you really that dumb? Did you really believe that crap about parents?'

She seemed to be playing some kind of game, to avoid going home.

'The lawyers I mentioned are a very old firm,' I assured her. 'They don't indulge in games.'

'I'll bet,' she scoffed. 'Old firm, huh? Gullible too, I'll bet. Tell you what, did they ask my old white-haired daddy to prove who he was?'

'Well — '

'Well nothing,' she finished. 'They've been had, brother. You've been had. Parents? My old lady died in a mental institution, and my father got shot in a bank raid, years back. I'll tell you who hired your lawyer buddies. They were family, all right. But not that kind, not the blood relative kind. The Halsetti family, that's who. You were supposed to take me home, right? Then they could have me quietly knocked off.'

My mind was in top gear, trying to adjust to what she was telling me.

'You're not quite right there,' I corrected. 'They said I was to take you back if you were willing. If not, they would come down here and — '

Even as I was trying to correct her, I could follow the rest of her argument. My voice tailed away.

Angela nodded.

'I see I'm getting through to you. All you had to do was to put the finger on me. Then they could send goons down to get rid of me.'

I shrugged, giving up.

'All right,' I admitted. 'Maybe I've been had, as you say. It's possible. But I still don't understand any of it. Why? Why would anybody want to harm you?'

She shook her head in wonderment.

'Are you really that stupid, or is this an act? You mean you haven't figured any of this out?'

'Partly,' I claimed. 'I know that Halsetti and Luckman were using you in a blackmail racket. I knew that somebody killed them, so as to get their hands on the gold. Then they killed the manager at the Almira — tell me, how did you manage to get away?'

'Get away?' she echoed dreamily, as if her mind was far off.

'From the apartment,' I insisted, 'after

250

Milton got shot. You must have been hurt, too. There was blood on one of your shirts.'

But she seemed to have lost interest.

'What were you doing with the rocks?' she demanded. 'That cosmic sculpture, or whatever.'

There was no point in my telling a tale, even if I'd seen a need. Where I had scraped away the paint, the gold was plain to see, on the most casual inspection.

'That,' I told her, 'is what this is all about. That pile of rocks is solid gold. There's half a million dollars sitting in that window.'

The greed made unattractive lines on that young face.

'So that's it,' she muttered, 'that's what the bastard meant. Luckman. He used to say 'some people can't see what's under their noses', then he'd laugh. No wonder. Well, he didn't get the last laugh.'

I could see she was having difficulty in restraining herself from going across to touch the gold. But that would have meant taking her eyes off me, and she didn't yet trust me enough.

I sat still in my chair. Angela stared at me thoughtfully for long seconds before speaking again.

'Make a deal with you,' she murmured. 'That stuff is too heavy for me to shift by myself. Besides, a girl needs a man around in this world. We'll split. What do you say? You get half the gold, and me. It's a fair offer. We could live in style on half a million.'

'We?' I repeated foolishly. 'Listen Angela, the life you've been leading has twisted your mind. Not all men are like that. I couldn't do it. I couldn't lay hands on a fourteen year old kid.'

'Fourteen?' she sneered. 'Is that what's bothering you? Well, forget it. I'm twenty six years old.'

It was a ridiculous claim, and my face must have said so. She clucked with impatience. 'You don't believe me?'

'Well,' I hedged, 'your face — '

'My face was an accident. I got caught in a fire, and there was a whole lot of face damage. The insurance company put this plastic surgeon onto me. Usual stuff. Skingrafts and all that. He did a good job,

252

too. I looked real good, just like I look now. That's the trouble. Seems there are certain muscles in your face, they control your skin movements. This butcher killed some of them. It was a cut-rate job, I guess. I'll always look the way I do right this minute. My neck is the giveaway. See?'

She pulled open the top of her blouse, and turned her head away.

There was no doubting it. The skin around the neck, although flawless, was certainly not that of an early teenager. As time went on, that skin would crease and fold. It would sag, and her face would remain the same. It was uncanny. For some reason, I shivered.

If Angela noticed, she gave no sign. Buttoning up the blouse with her free hand, she said

'Well, do we have a deal?'

'What if I refuse?'

'You know the answer to that,' she shrugged. 'I'll have to kill you, too.'

'Like you did Benny and the others?'

I knew the answer, but I wanted to hear her say it.

'Benny was a little bum, a real creep. Things had been getting too hot for us up-state, so he said we'd come down here and team up with his old pal, Luckman. Trouble was, they gave me the short end when it came to the dough. I went to work on old George, told him we didn't need Benny in the act. He kept promising to take care of him, but he didn't come through so I got tired of waiting. I did it myself.'

'You shot Benny?'

'Just said so, didn't I? You look just the way George did when I told him.'

She was so casual, so matter-of-fact about the whole thing that I knew she wouldn't hesitate to add me to the list.

'Why did you kill Luckman?'

She made a face.

'I always meant to, once I located this gold he had. But he forced me to it. When I told him about Benny, he like to went crazy. He wanted nothing to do with it, nothing to do with me.' She smiled emptily. 'Guess I over-estimated my power over old George. It didn't run to murder. So I had to kill him before time.

He was going to turn me loose, and I knew what that meant. As soon as my back was turned he'd make a phone call. After that I was as good as dead. I didn't have any choice, you see?'

To her it was no more than simple logic.

'Why was he in his pajamas?'

'Oh that. We were due to make some movies that day. George was all ready to start shooting. Well, the way it turned out, I started shooting first.'

'So you went to the manager at the Almira, and begged him to hide you, because there were nasty men after you.' I was thinking aloud. 'They killed your poor daddy, and they wanted to kill you. Was that it?'

'It's close enough,' she agreed. 'I'd seen that fat slob licking his lips. I didn't think he'd be too hard to sell. Too bad for him.'

'But why did you have to kill him?'

'He started to smell money. All this chatter about the gold, and big rewards, it got to him. He'd had what he wanted from me, and the thought of the cash was too much for him. He'd served his purpose, anyway.'

'But your clothes?' I wondered. 'I saw blood on them.'

'It was his. He made a grab at me as he fell down. Made me feel nauseated, him smearing me like that.' She stood up straight. 'Well, that's enough of the chatter. What's it gonna be? You want some of that' — waving at the gold-pile — 'or some of this?'

'Put it down, lady.'

She snarled, finger tightening on the trigger as she swung towards Sam Thompson's voice. There was a sharp crack from the automatic in his hand, followed by a heavier explosion as Angela's falling gun went off. Then she was standing, weeping and cursing as she clutched a ruined shoulder.

There was cold sweat on my forehead.

'Where the hell have you been?' I demanded ungraciously.

'I been listening,' he replied easily. 'I'm what you might call a material witness. Heard the whole thing. Why did she point to that junk over there? What would you want with that?'

'I'll explain later,' I said wearily. 'Get some law.'

★ ★ ★

Late the next afternoon, I sat reading the midday editions. I got some fair publicity, but that was all. As to any reward, there was some clause that said nobody could collect if he found the gold in the course of his normal duties. That let me out.

I offered Mr. Gettysburg Andrews his check back, but to my surprise the old guy refused.

'No, no. In my view you are entitled to that money, Mr. Preston. You acted in good faith, as I did. And don't look upon this as a charitable gesture. It is nothing of the kind. The people who gave me my instructions may have deceived me, indeed they have deceived me. But if they imagine they are going to evade payment of all emoluments expended, believe me, they are deceiving themselves.'

Mr. Andrews, it would seem, was tougher than he looked.

The phone blatted, and a familiar

grating voice was on the other end.

'Preston? This is Keppler.'

Big Jule doesn't make many calls. I stared at the receiver.

'How're things, Jule?'

'Off and on,' he returned. 'Off and on. It says in the book here you're down for five Cs on the third tomorrow. Gee-gee's name is The Loser. Do I have it right?'

He knew damned well it was right. The point was, why the call?

'Oh the button,' I confirmed.

There was a pause.

'I got news for you,' he said grittily. 'At least I hope it's news. The nag is a switcheroo. The race track coppers are locking up everybody in sight.'

I swallowed.

'But this is terrible,' I protested. 'Could there be some mistake?'

'The only mistake I know about is your five centuries,' he replied. 'You know the rules.'

I knew the rules. No refunds. But it wouldn't sound good for me to lie down too easily.

'Now just a minute,' I blustered. 'I

made that bet in good faith — '

'Hope you did, Preston, I certainly hope you did. Anyway, it's what they call a natural sequence. They called the switch horse The Loser. You lost.'

The brr-ing noise announced that he'd hung up.

I did the same, staring glumly at the desk top. I was just a messenger boy. Mr. Andrews gave me five hundred dollars, I handed it straight to Jule Keppler.

Just like that.

The door opened, and Florence Digby came in.

'Thought you'd want to know at once. There's news of Horace Winters.'

I brightened. All was not lost. Horace Winters was good for fifteen hundred dollars cash money. Even in the course of my normal duties.

'Florence,' I assured her. 'You have my undivided attention. Where do I find old Horace?'

'They have him locked up down at the Seventh Precinct,' she returned sweetly. 'I thought you ought to know.'

Then she went away.

I went moodily across to the window, staring out.

Horace Winters was just the latest in a long line of losers, it seemed.

Maybe somebody was trying to tell me something.

THE END

We do hope that you have enjoyed reading this large print book.

Did you know that all of our titles are available for purchase?

We publish a wide range of high quality large print books including:
Romances, Mysteries, Classics
General Fiction
Non Fiction and Westerns

Special interest titles available in large print are:
The Little Oxford Dictionary
Music Book, Song Book
Hymn Book, Service Book

Also available from us courtesy of Oxford University Press:
Young Readers' Dictionary
(large print edition)
Young Readers' Thesaurus
(large print edition)

For further information or a free brochure, please contact us at:
Ulverscroft Large Print Books Ltd.,
The Green, Bradgate Road, Anstey,
Leicester, LE7 7FU, England.
Tel: (00 44) **0116 236 4325**
Fax: (00 44) **0116 234 0205**

Other titles in the
Linford Mystery Library:

DEATH CALLED AT NIGHT

R. A. Bennett

Jimmy Ellis believes his parents have died in a car crash when as a young boy he is taken to live with relatives in Australia. The years pass happily, then the nightmare comes. Terrifying images flit through his mind in the dark — all through the eyes of a child, a witness to grisly events seventeen years before. He begins to delve into the past, and soon he finds himself on the trail of a double murderer — a murderer who is prepared to kill again.

THE DEAD TALE-TELLERS

John Newton Chance

Jonathan Blake always kept appointments. He had kept many, in all sorts of places, at all sorts of times, but never one like that one he kept in the house in the woods in the fading light of an October day. It seemed a perfect, peaceful place to visit and perhaps take tea and muffins round the fire. But at this appointment his footsteps dragged, for he knew that inside the house the men with whom he had that date were already dead . . .

THREE DAYS TO LIVE

Robert Charles

Mike Harrigan was scar-faced, a drifter, and something of a woman-hater. With his partner Dan Barton he searched the upper reaches of the Rio Negro in the treacherous rain forests of Brazil, lured by a fortune in uncut emeralds. Behind them rode three killers who believed that they had already found the precious stones. And then fate handed Harrigan not emeralds, but the lives of women, three of them nuns, and trapped them all in a vast series of underground caverns.

TURN DOWN AN EMPTY GLASS

Basil Copper

L.A. private detective Mike Faraday is plunged into a bizarre web of Haitian voodoo and murder when the beautiful singer Jenny Lundquist comes to him in fear for her life. Staked out at the lonely Obelisk Point, Mike sees the sinister Legba, the voodoo god of the crossroads, with his cane and straw sack. But Mike discovers that beneath the superstition and an apparently motiveless series of appalling crimes is an ingenious plot — with a multi-million dollar prize.

DEATH IN RETREAT

George Douglas

On a day of retreat for clergy at Overdale House, a resident guest, Martin Pender, is foully murdered. The primary task of the Regional Homicide Squad is to track down the bogus parson who joined the retreat. Subsequent events show that serious political motives lie behind the killing, but the basic lead to it all is missing. Then, three young tearaways corner the killer in the woods, and a chess problem, set out on a board, yields vital evidence.